From their position on the hillside, Nancy and Frank watched as the two runners entered the final stretch. The road ran along the bottom of a high canyon wall, and eroded sandstone cliffs towered above them.

Suddenly Cory spurted forward. The distance between him and Tasio opened briefly. Tasio ran harder.

"Go for it!" Frank exclaimed, raising his fist in the air. The gap between the two runners closed with Tasio's sudden burst of speed. They were neck and neck.

Then a glint of sunlight on something shiny drew Nancy's eyes to the canyon rim high above the road. She saw a cloud of dust and a car driving away from the rim at great speed. Something wasn't right. She froze when she saw what was happening.

A huge boulder was rushing down the side of the canyon—right toward Tasio Humada and Cory Weston!

Nancy Drew & Hardy Boys SuperMysteries

Available from ARCHWAY Paperbacks

For orders other than by individual consumers, Archway Books grants a discount on the purchase of **10 or more** copies of single titles for special markets or premium use. For further details, please write to the Vice-President of Special Markets, Pocket Books, 1230 Avenue of the Americas, New York, NY 10020.

For information on how individual consumers can place orders, please write to Mail Order Department, Paramount Publishing, 200 Old Tappan Road, Old Tappan, NJ 07675.

A NANCY DREW and HARDY BOYS

SUPER·MYSTERY™

COPPER CANYON CONSPIRACY

Carolyn Keene

AN ARCHWAY PAPERBACK
Published by POCKET BOOKS
New York   London   Toronto   Sydney   Tokyo   Singapore

This book is a work of fiction. Names, characters, places and incidents are products of the author's imagination or are used fictitiously. Any resemblance to actual events or locales or persons, living or dead, is entirely coincidental.

AN ARCHWAY PAPERBACK *Original*

 An Archway Paperback published by
POCKET BOOKS, a division of Simon & Schuster Inc.
1230 Avenue of the Americas, New York, NY 10020

Copyright © 1994 by Simon & Schuster Inc.
Produced by Mega-Books, Inc.

ISBN: 0-671-88514-6

First Archway Paperback printing December 1994

10 9 8 7 6 5 4 3 2 1

NANCY DREW, THE HARDY BOYS, AN ARCHWAY PAPERBACK and colophon are registered trademarks of Simon & Schuster Inc.

A NANCY DREW AND HARDY BOYS SUPERMYSTERY is a trademark of Simon & Schuster Inc.

Cover art by Vince Natale

Printed in the U.S.A.

IL 6+

COPPER CANYON
CONSPIRACY

Chapter

One

H E'S LOOKING this way again," Nancy Drew murmured to her friend George Fayne for the third time in five minutes.

Nancy's bright blue eyes glinted mischievously as a teasing smile played at the corners of her mouth. She had noticed the tall, handsome, sandy-haired young man flashing George a quick, friendly smile when they first arrived near the starting line of the Cactus Marathon, a twenty-six-mile race held in Tucson, Arizona. He was tall and lanky, and even from thirty feet away Nancy could see that his eyes were a brilliant blue. He couldn't seem to stop checking out George.

"Too bad you already have a boyfriend," George said casually.

"He's interested in you, not me, one-oh-nine," Nancy said, referring to the number George was wearing. Smiling, she added, "And unless you're hiding something from me, you're available."

George didn't respond, concentrating instead on her warm-up exercises.

As George stretched, Nancy studied the huge shopping center parking lot where the starting line was located. Nancy estimated the crowd at a thousand people, most in jogging attire. Blue police barricades divided the starting area from traffic, and from a long line of cars more runners were being dropped off for the event.

Nancy was glad she had worn shorts, a white cotton blouse, and sandals. The desert sun burned down on them. It was going to be hot.

Nancy noticed George cast another quick glance in the direction of the sandy-haired guy, who was wearing number 71. Simultaneously he turned and caught George's eye. Unlike most of the other runners, who were surrounded by friends, Nancy noticed that he was alone. He waved at George and gave her a friendly smile before jogging in their direction.

George started blushing.

"Hi! I'm Cory Weston," the young man said cheerfully as he approached. "Are you from Tucson?"

"I'm George Fayne. And this is my friend

Nancy Drew," George replied. "We came all the way from River Heights, Illinois."

"Cool," Cory said. "I'm from a little closer, a ranch outside Bisbee, Arizona. It's near the Mexican border, about two hours southeast of here."

"I hope I do okay in the marathon," George said. "I'm not used to running twenty-five hundred feet above sea level. I know being this high can really slow you down if you're not used to it. But I guess that's no problem for you."

Cory laughed. "Our ranch is at about five thousand feet, and I do most of my practicing on the gravel roads around where I live. So, yeah, I guess you could say I'm used to the altitude. But the heat still gets to me. And it's supposed to hit eighty-five."

George groaned. Nancy held up the plastic water bottle. "Don't worry, George, there'll be lots of water along the way."

"Those are the runners to watch," Cory said, pointing toward the starting line. Five young men with long, black hair and dark, copper-colored skin stood together, talking quietly. They wore shorts and T-shirts. Short in stature, their arms and legs rippled with muscles.

Nancy noticed Cory's obvious admiration of them. "They're Tarahumara Indians," he explained. "They'll beat us all, and they won't even be breathing hard when they're finished."

"Tarahumara?" Nancy asked. "A friend of my father, an anthropologist, is sponsoring them at this race. We're supposed to keep an eye out for him."

"You don't mean Dr. Bingham Stone, do you?" Cory asked.

"Yes!" Nancy exclaimed. "Do you know him?"

Cory paused. He seemed to be searching for an answer. "By reputation," he said finally. "He sponsored some Tara runners last year, too."

"Why are they such good runners?" George asked, gazing at the line of young men.

"Running is part of their culture," Cory explained. "In fact, the name of their tribe means 'the people who run.' They come from the Copper Canyon region of northern Mexico, and stories about Tarahumara races are legendary. They can go for hours, up and down rugged mountains, without ever breaking pace."

Just then Nancy saw something that stunned her. "They're not wearing running shoes! Are they going to run in their bare feet?"

Cory grinned. "I've read that the soles of their feet are as tough as tree bark. Running shoes would probably give them blisters."

"And they win marathons that way?" George asked, incredulous.

"Not always," Cory said. "Some Tarahumaras have raced in the Olympic Games, but not all

4

that successfully. They complain that the marathon is too short. They run for different reasons than we do—like delivering messages—sometimes with packs on their backs over great distances. So they consider twenty-six miles too short."

"What does Dr. Stone look like?" George asked Nancy. "Do you see him?"

"Dad said he's tall and has a gray beard," Nancy replied. "Maybe we should go over and ask the Tarahumara runners if they know where he is."

"Speaking of people we can't find," George said, "what happened to Frank and Joe?"

Their close friends Frank and Joe Hardy had accompanied Nancy and George to Tucson because Joe was also competing. Nancy and Frank's job was to support George and Joe with water, foot massages, and blister care.

George turned to Cory. "We're supposed to meet our friends at the starting line this morning. I'm running with a guy named Joe."

"Is he your boyfriend?" Cory asked with a disarming smile.

George laughed. "Oh, no," she said quickly. "We're just good friends."

"George isn't seeing anyone special these days," Nancy interjected, giving her friend a wink.

George blushed and changed the subject. She

stood on her tiptoes, and with the flat of her hand shading her brow, searched the crowd. "I hope we can find the Hardys."

Although they lived far from Nancy, on the East Coast, Frank and Joe Hardy had a lot in common with her. They were all successful sleuths, and quite a few times the friends had joined forces to solve mysteries.

Nancy heard a familiar voice behind her. "There are the best-looking girls in Arizona!"

When Nancy turned, she saw Joe Hardy jogging toward them, dodging other runners. The bright sunlight glinted off his blond hair. Joe wore gray shorts, dirty white sneakers, and a baggy, faded green T-shirt that was so old and full of holes it barely held together on his stocky, muscular torso. Behind him, his dark-haired older brother, Frank, sauntered along at a more leisurely pace.

"How do you keep the fans away?" Joe teased after he'd stopped beside them.

"Very funny," George said, turning to Cory as Frank Hardy came up behind Joe. "Cory, these are our friends Frank and Joe Hardy." Turning to the Hardys, she said, "This is Cory Weston. He's from Bisbee, a town south of here."

Cory shook hands with both of them. "Actually, I live on a cattle ranch."

Joe looked suddenly intrigued. "Does that mean you're a cowboy?"

Cory threw back his head and laughed. "Well, when I'm not racing I wear a Stetson and drive a pickup truck, so yeah, I guess I am. George says that you're running, too."

The younger Hardy nodded with obvious pride. "And I'm doing it in three hours," he said confidently. "George, too. We thought we'd run together and pace each other."

Nancy saw Cory's eyes light up. "That's my goal, too. Maybe we can— I mean if you don't mind, maybe I could run with you."

Joe looked at George. "No problem with me."

George smiled at Cory. "Great idea," she said. "We may as well share our misery."

"We should see if we can find Dr. Stone before the marathon starts," Nancy suggested.

"That anthropologist friend of your dad?" Joe asked.

Nancy nodded and pointed toward the starting line on the other side of the police barricades. "Those are the Tarahumaras. I should go over and ask if they know where Dr. Stone is."

Nancy started toward the Indian runners, with the others following. As she approached, she saw one of them step out in front. He was slightly taller than the others—although still only about five-ten. He saw Nancy approaching, and she watched him scrutinize her, his head tilted at a slight angle.

"Hi!" she called out when she was only a few

feet away. "I'm Nancy Drew, and my father's a friend of Dr. Bingham Stone. I'm supposed to look him up. Do you know—"

"Bing!" the young man said, his face lighting up. To Nancy, he sounded like any American kid, especially the way he called Dr. Stone by a nickname. "*Sí,* we know Bing."

By this time the eyes of all the Tarahumara runners were on Nancy. The tall one turned and spoke to the others in his own language. One, wearing a red bandanna around his head, rapidly replied. The tall one turned back to her.

"My name is Tasio Humada." He gestured to the man with the red bandanna. "And my friend Chacho says Bing had to take care of some business but will be here soon."

Chacho gave Nancy a wide, friendly smile. Tasio extended his hand, and Nancy clasped it firmly. The Tarahumara's hand was limp in hers, making it, at most, a lukewarm greeting. His gaze, however, was so intense that Nancy found it unsettling.

"I'm with some friends," Nancy said a little awkwardly. The others had caught up and were waiting beside her. Cory Weston held back, as if unsure whether to join the group. Nancy introduced everyone.

Tasio beamed as he gestured to the other Tarahumara runners, naming them one by one.

"My friends Chacho, Patricio, Celedonio, and Vitorio."

Just then an announcer's voice boomed through the sound system, amid a loud, blood-curdling screech and a burst of static. Nancy glanced at her watch.

"It's three minutes to eight," she announced. "I guess they're asking everyone to take their places. We'll have to look for Dr. Stone during the race."

She was interrupted by Frank, shouting, "Look out!"

Nancy spun around just as she heard the screech of rubber on pavement, a loud crash, and splintering wood. Cory was behind her, and Tasio stood beside him, as a runaway car smashed through the wooden police barricades, heading straight toward them!

Chapter

Two

Nancy tackled George and Cory to push them out of the way. The three of them crashed to the pavement just as a dull green car sped over the spot where they had been standing only seconds before. The rear end of the car fishtailed as the driver turned sharply. Simultaneously, Frank and Joe had shoved Tasio and the other Tarahumaras out of the way. They barely escaped being hit as the car headed back through the broken barricades.

Lifting her head, Nancy saw panic-stricken runners scattering. She jumped to her feet and squinted to read the license plate of the car. The vehicle tore around parked cars and veered onto the street.

Joe Hardy ran to Nancy. "Are you all right?" he asked.

Nancy grimaced. "I'm going to have black-and-blue knees," she said. "But I'm okay. I tried to get the license number, but I missed it."

"Whoever's driving that thing is crazy!" Frank exclaimed, joining them.

George and Cory were brushing themselves off, with the help of some other runners.

"Are you guys okay?" Nancy asked.

George glanced at her palms, where the skin had been scraped raw. "At least I don't need my hands for the marathon." She sighed. "And so much for wearing all white," she said, giving a final brush to her T-shirt and shorts.

"Let's find a first-aid station and get some antiseptic on those cuts," Cory suggested.

Nancy noticed the Tarahumaras' smiles were gone. They eyed the crowd suspiciously and moved away from people who wanted to express concern.

On the avenue next to the parking lot, a white police car screamed past, its red and blue lights flashing, its siren blaring. Several enterprising runners commandeered a barricade from somewhere else and replaced the broken one.

The announcer's voice came over the P.A. system again, stating a temporary delay in the starting time. "If you're dropping off runners," the voice boomed loudly, "remember the speed limit is five miles an hour! We just about lost some runners because someone was driving too fast and lost control!"

"Lost control—right," Joe said. "That was deliberate."

Frank shook his head dubiously at his younger brother. "That's how my brother gets his exercise," he said to Nancy. "Jumping to conclusions."

Before Nancy could respond, Joe said, "You're wrong, Frank—unless, of course, the guy's gas pedal was stuck. But I still say it was deliberate."

While Joe was talking, Nancy noticed a tall, gray-haired man with ruddy skin and a closely clipped gray beard approach Tasio and the other Tarahumaras. She moved closer to the group. The man was obviously worried. The Tarahumaras greeted him like an old friend, and then Tasio spoke to him. The older man turned toward Nancy and strode toward her.

"Miss Drew!" he said formally, extending his hand. "I'm Bingham Stone. Your dad telephoned me to tell me you were here for the marathon. Are you all right?"

"Yes, fine," Nancy assured him, shaking his hand.

"I don't know what to say," Dr. Stone told her apologetically. "I know it sounds silly, but I almost feel responsible."

"That's nonsense," Nancy insisted. "It had nothing to do with you. No one was hurt, so we can all be thankful for that."

Dr. Stone leaned closer and spoke quickly in a low, urgent voice. "That speeding car may have been a deliberate attempt on Tasio's life."

Nancy was momentarily taken aback. "What makes you think——"

"Someone has been sending him threatening letters," Dr. Stone whispered. "The Taras are staying with me here at my home in Tucson, and a letter was delivered to the house last night. I tried to persuade Tasio not to run, but he refuses to pull out."

"Do the police know?" Nancy asked.

Dr. Stone glanced about as if he was afraid of being overheard. "Carson told me that you're a very successful young detective. He suggested that we talk alone—after the race."

Before Nancy could reply, she saw Frank, Joe, and George approaching. Nancy introduced her friends. Then, noticing that Cory was hanging back again, she caught Dr. Stone's attention. "And this is a new friend," she told the anthropologist. "Cory Weston."

"Weston!" Dr. Stone uttered in astonishment. He stared at Cory as if sizing him up.

"It's a pleasure to meet you, Dr. Stone," the young runner said without real friendliness.

"I've, um, heard about your work with the Tarahumaras in Mexico."

"Are you related to Marcus Weston at the Double W Ranch?" Dr. Stone demanded.

Cory nodded. "He's my dad."

"I see," Stone said sharply. Abruptly, he strode back to the Tarahumaras. Nancy was taken aback by his rudeness, and she was aware of Cory's embarrassment.

The awkward moment ended when two officials from the marathon committee approached, clipboards in hand. They took down everyone's name and asked if anyone could identify the car.

"You bet," Frank asserted. "An old Plymouth. Dull green with a brown front fender on the passenger side, and a single whitewall tire on the rear passenger side."

"License plate?" one of the officials asked, jotting the information down.

"It was white," Nancy offered. "With green numbers. But I couldn't make them out."

"Hmmm," the official said. "Sounds like it might've been from Sonora."

"That's the Mexican state just south of the border," Cory explained.

"Any word from the police?" Joe asked. "I saw a cruiser take off after the car."

"We'll let you know," the official said. "If they press charges for reckless driving, we might need

14

you in court. We're very sorry about this. I hope you enjoy the rest of the Cactus Marathon."

"If it ever begins," George said, not bothering to mask the exasperation in her voice.

The official laughed. "It will. In about five minutes." With that, the two officials strode back to the long row of tables near the starting line, where other officials were gathered.

The Tarahumaras were clustered around Dr. Stone, not far away. The anthropologist separated himself from them and walked back to Nancy. "I must take care of my charges," he said. "Will you excuse me? After the race I hope you'll have the opportunity to meet them again. They're extraordinary athletes. When they hunt, they can run down wild turkey or deer."

"We'd love to," Nancy volunteered on everyone's behalf. "We're staying at the Saguaro Inn. We can meet there later." She gave Dr. Stone a smile. "And have a chat."

The voice over the loudspeaker announced the start of the marathon in three minutes and issued a final call for runners to take their positions.

"We'll meet you at the five-mile mark," Nancy said to George and Joe.

"Well, at least running a marathon is a great way to work off the tension from almost being killed," George said.

"It might even make you run faster," Nancy said cheerfully. "Good luck!"

Joe, George, and Cory headed toward the starting line, forty feet away. Nancy and Frank moved to a position on the sidelines. A hush fell over the crowd of runners as they waited for the sound of the cannon.

Boom!

Nancy felt the vibrations from the loud report through the ground under her feet.

"They're off!" Frank shouted.

The tightly packed crowd of runners surged forward across the starting line. Already several top runners had pulled out in front, but an early lead didn't mean victory. Some of the runners in front might tire quickly, and some might not even finish the race.

"There are Joe and George!" Nancy called out, waving as they ran past. Joe was slightly in the lead, with George and Cory Weston flanking him.

Not far behind them, she saw the Tarahumara runners, jogging together at a rather slow, even pace. Runners were surging around them like water rushing in a stream and parting around a stone. To Nancy, the Tarahumaras seemed oblivious to the palpable tension and excitement in the air.

"We should get going," Frank said. "I don't know my way around Tucson. If we get lost, Joe and George will get to the five-mile mark before we do."

Joe and George had planned a series of quick stops every five miles. Nancy and Frank were to meet them at each stop, with high-energy drinks and water. If either Joe or George flagged behind, Nancy and Frank were to wait before going on to the next five-mile point.

Frank found the five-mile checkpoint easily, although they had to detour around streets that were blocked off.

They had to park almost half a mile from the meeting place, a park along the banks of the Santa Cruz River. Nancy found the park strangely beautiful. It was flat and covered with tall, yellow grasses and fine sand. The cement fence that ran along the road was decorated with beautiful glazed tiles.

Frank grabbed the backpack filled with water and energy drinks, while Nancy carried a small first-aid kit, equipped for blisters.

"Swim?" Frank suggested, gesturing toward the river as they walked toward the five-mile checkpoint. The Santa Cruz River was bone dry, a winding ribbon of gravel.

"It's hard to think of it as a river," Nancy said. "I read in a brochure that a hundred years ago it ran with water all year round."

"Oh, yeah? What happened?"

"Apparently people put in wells to grow cotton and pecans and oranges, and the water table fell a hundred feet. So all the mesquite forests died, and the rivers are dry except when it rains or the snow melts," Nancy explained.

Frank sighed. "It shows what can happen when people tamper with the environment too much."

They heard a loud cheer rise from the hundreds of people gathered near the checkpoint ahead of them. There was a large tent with a Red Cross banner indicating it was for medical services. Tables covered with water jugs lined the marathon route, staffed by volunteers who stood ready with paper cups to hand to the runners as they went by.

The road was still deserted. The runners hadn't reached that point yet, but when Frank and Nancy craned their necks to see beyond the crowd, the first runner jogged into view. Almost immediately he was followed by another, then another. A roar went up from the crowd.

Nancy and Frank pushed their way to the edge of the road and waited. Several dozen runners went by, and then Joe, George, and Cory—all three still running together—came into view.

As they drew closer, Nancy noticed Joe's T-shirt was plastered to his chest with sweat. Cory, however, seemed as fresh as he had at the start of the race.

"Whew, hot," Joe said as he slowed. Nancy and Frank jogged alongside. Frank twisted open a bottle of water and handed it to Joe. Joe held it over his head and turned it upside down. The contents fell in a clear stream over his blond hair and down his face. He sighed. "Oh, man, I needed that."

Meanwhile, George slowed, too, as she neared, took the bottle of energy drink that Nancy offered her, and started drinking immediately.

Nancy dug into the knapsack and offered Cory a bottle. "Thanks. I can use it," he said, barely slowing down. Cory, she realized, didn't want to waste a second. Jogging beside the three runners, Nancy held up the first-aid kit.

"Bandage brigade," she announced. "Anyone need one?"

"So far so good," Joe said, glancing at his beat-up training shoes. "How about you, Georgie?" he teased.

"No problem, kiddo," George shot back, and outpaced him.

Just then Frank shouted excitedly, "There are the Tarahumaras!"

"Tasio runs as if he were speed itself," Nancy remarked, still jogging along beside her friends.

Tasio and Chacho were ahead of the other Taras. Tasio's dark eyes were focused like a beam of light on the road ahead. To Nancy, he seemed barely aware of the other runners, the tables of refreshments, or the spectators lining the road.

George interrupted Nancy's thoughts by abruptly tossing back the rest of her drink over her shoulder.

Cory tossed his drink, too, and Nancy found herself holding two half-empty bottles.

Joe tossed his emptied bottle into a nearby trash can as if he were shooting a basket. It landed perfectly. "Today, I'm on!" he declared, bolting after George and Cory. Nancy and Frank slowed and came to a stop in the milling crowd.

The morning went by a lot faster than Nancy had expected. It grew increasingly warmer as the sun burned its way across the desert sky. Some of the marathon runners began to drop out. At the ten-mile checkpoint, Nancy saw ambulances carting away a few runners who had suffered heat prostration.

Frank and Nancy reached the fifteen-mile checkpoint just in time to spot Cory running past. They offered him water and a bandage for a blister developing on his left heel. Cory took off after only a few moments, and then Joe appeared. He poured a bottle of water over his head and slurped down half a bottle of energy drink while continuing to race.

Nancy and Frank waited for George, who appeared a minute later just ahead of the bulk of the runners. Although George had fallen behind Cory and Joe, she was definitely holding her own, Nancy thought. George also needed a bandage and spent precious seconds putting it on. Then she was gone.

Frank and Nancy reached the twenty-mile checkpoint just as the first runners were going past.

"Look, there's Cory!" Nancy exclaimed. "It looks like he's in third place!"

Cory spotted them and lifted one arm in a quick, weary wave.

"And Tasio and Chacho are fourth and fifth," Frank said, pointing to the next two runners coming down the road.

Nancy's eyes widened when she saw the two Tarahumaras. They were running at an astonishing speed, their bare feet pounding the road. Fifteen minutes later Joe arrived at the twenty-mile mark, with George less than thirty feet behind him. She looked tired, but she had kept pace with Joe.

Joe doused himself under another bottle of water and helped George out by emptying a bottle over her head as well.

"Feels fabulous!" George panted as they ran.

With the Cactus Marathon's third hour almost up, Frank and Nancy headed for the finish line, in a park at Sabino Canyon, a recreation area at the foot of the Catalina Mountains on Tucson's north side. This, they both knew, was going to be the acid test for the marathoners. It was almost noon, and the temperature was well into the eighties. To get to Sabino Canyon, the marathoners had to run uphill.

At the spot where Frank and Nancy left their rented car, the Catalina Mountains towered above them. "Let's climb up there," Nancy said, pointing to an outcropping of rock nearby. "We'll see everyone get to the finish line."

They scaled the steep hillside, and when they reached the outcropping, they discovered a perfect view of the road as it approached the canyon.

Nancy spotted George because she was one of the tallest women runners. She was far back from the front runners but racing almost even with Joe and three other women.

"Joe's flagging," Frank commented. "George conserved energy by keeping her speed down for the first ten miles. Now she's pouring it on."

Nancy scanned the front runners. "There's Cory Weston!" she exclaimed. Only a dozen runners were ahead of him.

"Tasio's right beside him," Frank added.

Sure enough, the Tarahumara runner was almost even with Cory Weston. Nancy spotted Chacho some thirty feet behind Tasio. Cory and Tasio were straining to maintain their speed. As they crested the slope, Tasio started to pull ahead.

From their position on the hillside, Nancy and Frank watched as the two runners entered the final stretch. The road ran along the bottom of a high canyon wall, and eroded sandstone cliffs towered above them. Suddenly, Cory spurted ahead of Tasio. The distance between them opened briefly. Tasio ran harder.

"Go for it!" Frank exclaimed, raising his fist in the air. The gap between the two runners closed. They were neck and neck.

Then a glint of sunlight on something shiny drew Nancy's eyes to the canyon rim high above the road. She saw a cloud of dust swirling rapidly in the air and a car driving away from the rim at great speed. Something wasn't right. She froze when she saw what was happening.

A huge boulder was rushing down the side of the canyon—right toward Tasio Humada and Cory Weston!

Chapter

Three

NANCY FELT POWERLESS to do anything as the boulder plummeted down.

"Watch out!" Frank yelled instinctively, and reached out to grip Nancy's arm.

Just above the road, the boulder hit an outcropping, slowed, bounced, and then continued falling. Tasio and Cory were right in its path. At the last possible second Cory Weston saw the boulder.

Nancy and Frank watched helplessly as Cory smashed sideways into Tasio, throwing the runner away from the deadly boulder. Cory wasn't so lucky.

The boulder smashed against Cory, knocking him down. Tasio was pushing himself up from the road, and Chacho, who had just come over the slope of the hill, was rushing to his side. Other runners, determined not to let a mishap disrupt their racing time, passed by in an endless flow.

"Let's go," Frank said, grabbing Nancy's hand.

They half slid, half ran down the hillside, scattering stones and pebbles. When they reached the scene of the accident, Cory was still on the ground, with Tasio and Chacho kneeling beside him. Nancy saw a bright red stain on Cory's running shoe. His face was white, but he was smiling bravely. The boulder lay on the road like a humongous dinosaur egg.

"He saved my life," Tasio told Nancy simply.

"Are you okay?" Nancy asked Cory, kneeling beside him. "What hurts the most?"

"The lower part of my left leg feels like a bulldozer ran over it," he said. He winced as he gestured toward his bloody running shoe. "Guess I'm not going to finish the marathon," he said matter-of-factly.

"I guess not," Frank seconded.

They heard a few short, shrill blasts and turned to see an ambulance slowly making its way through the stream of runners.

Three paramedics in white uniforms hopped out from the back of the ambulance. Two slid a folded-up gurney from the back of the vehicle and began to assemble it, while the other sprinted to Cory's side. Deftly, he splinted Cory's left leg from his thigh to his ankle.

On the downslope of the hill, Joe Hardy panted hard, pounding out the last mile of the marathon. He saw the commotion as he crested the final hill. When he realized who was at the center of it, he pulled over.

Nancy and Frank greeted him glumly and explained what had happened.

"Any idea where George is?" Nancy asked.

Joe struggled to catch his breath. Nancy noted that his face was beet red. "No," Joe said, "I pulled ahead about twenty minutes ago, and I haven't seen her since." He noticed Tasio, who was staring silently at Cory. "Are you all right?" Joe asked.

Tasio nodded calmly. "This marathon was not meant to be finished," he stated. Then he added, "Yes, I am all right. Cory pushed me away from the boulder, and it hit him instead."

"Slammed into my leg and rolled right over it," Cory muttered. The paramedic signaled to the men with the gurney.

"You really think I need an ambulance to go to the hospital?" Cory protested halfheartedly.

The paramedic smiled as he helped the other two attendants carefully lift Cory onto the gurney. "Well, you sure can't walk to the medical center," he said. "And you have to get this x-rayed."

Nancy motioned Frank and Joe aside and spoke quietly to them. "This might sound weird, but I know I saw a car up there"—she pointed up the canyon wall—"just before that rock fell."

"Another hit and run, so to speak?" Joe asked.

Nancy and Frank exchanged glances. "It's possible," Frank said grimly.

"There's something else," Nancy said quickly. "When Dr. Stone heard about the reckless driver, he told me that Tasio has been getting death threats. Apparently, a letter to Tasio was delivered to Dr. Stone's home last night."

"So it *is* deliberate!" Joe exclaimed.

"We can't know for sure until we look around on top of that cliff," Nancy said.

"I think we should go with Cory to the hospital," Frank pointed out.

"I'll go with him," Joe volunteered. "My time on the marathon is all messed up now anyway. And I'm beat. The last thing I want to do is go on an expedition to the top of this canyon. I'll finish the Cactus Marathon next year."

Nancy smiled sympathetically. "You would have made it in three hours," she said, quickly calculating how long it might have taken Joe to run the last half mile.

Joe beamed. "On a hot day and in the mountains, too."

Just then George ran up. "What's going on?" she gasped. Quickly, Nancy explained.

The paramedics were pushing the gurney toward the ambulance. Tasio still hovered at Cory's side, and Chacho was nearby with the other Tarahumaras. The Hardys, Nancy, and George joined the others.

"Oh, Cory, I'm so sorry," George said, running up to him. She was breathing heavily, and her sweatband was soaked. "I'll go to the hospital with you."

Cory looked at George. "Finish the race," he said firmly. "I know your times are off, but do it for me. I'm not able to finish."

"Don't be silly," George told him. "I'm going with you."

"That's okay, George," Joe interjected. "I'm throwing in the towel. I'll go with Cory and bring him back to our bed-and-breakfast when the doctors have finished dissecting him."

"Thanks, Joe," Cory said. He turned his head to George and said softly, "I mean it, George. It's only another half mile. Go for it."

Cory turned to Tasio and the other Tarahumaras. "You guys should finish, too," he urged. "Why don't all of you finish the last half mile together. For me."

"And for me, too," Joe said.

Tasio's eyes met George's. "Will you run with us?" he invited.

"I'd love to!" George exclaimed. She turned to Nancy and Frank. "I'll get a lift to the hotel after the race and meet you back there."

Tasio gripped Cory's wrist. "I will see you later, my friend," he said. The paramedics loaded the gurney into the ambulance.

George and Nancy hugged quickly. Then George was off, running in the center of the Tarahumara runners. Joe climbed into the ambulance, and it moved slowly back through the traffic of runners.

Nancy stared up at the face of the cliff. "There has to be a road that goes up there."

"Not necessarily," Frank said. "The person might have been driving a four-wheel-drive Jeep or truck."

"No," Nancy said. "It was a dull green car—and it was old."

"Dull green!" Frank exclaimed. "That was the color of the car that nearly hit Tasio and Cory."

"You're right!" Nancy said excitedly. "I was concentrating so hard on trying to get the license plate earlier that I didn't pay attention to the color of the car."

"Well, then," Frank said, "there has to be a road up there. That car wouldn't have made it otherwise."

Frank glanced down the road. Around them the runners kept jogging past, but many appeared to be at the point of exhaustion. He noticed a sign in the distance and what looked like a trail up the side of the canyon. "Let's check that out," he suggested.

When he and Nancy got close enough, they saw a sign for the Old Soldier Trail, with a symbol for hikers.

They scaled the path quickly, finding that after the first steep ascent of about twenty feet, it hugged a narrow ridge along the side of the canyon, and suddenly they found themselves at the rim of the canyon, where a gravel road ran out into desert.

"This way," Nancy said, pointing in the direction where she'd seen the glint of sunlight on metal. She and Frank followed the road for only a minute, until they reached a flat, stony outcropping.

Nancy spotted tire tracks in the sand between the rocks. "Frank, look at these tracks!" she exclaimed. "They must have been made recently. There's enough of a wind up here that tracks left in sand would vanish in a matter of hours." She sighed. "Unfortunately, tracks don't prove anything."

"Look over there," Frank said. He pointed to the edge of the outcropping. "Footprints."

Nancy saw a patch of sand that had been swept by rain into a dune against the edge of a boulder, then washed flat. As she and Frank approached, she made out two sets of prints.

From there they had a clear view down to the road below. They could see workers placing bright orange cones around the fallen rock and the other debris that had rolled down the hill with it. At the edge of the cliff there was a large, almost circular spot of bald ground, lighter in color than the surrounding area.

"That's where the boulder was originally!" Nancy exclaimed. "That bare spot looks about the same size."

"And what's this?" Frank said. He knelt to examine a long, rusty iron rod on the ground several feet away. It was similar to the kind used to reinforce concrete. One end of the iron rod had been scraped, revealing gleaming metal beneath the rusty surface.

Nancy leaned over Frank's shoulder. "Someone must have used it as a lever to pry the boulder over the edge."

"And they had a clear view over the hill of who was coming next," Nancy noted. "So they knew it was Tasio."

"Or Cory," Frank pointed out. "If this is connected to the speeding car, both times Cory and Tasio happened to be together."

Nancy thought for a moment. "Maybe it's just some joker trying to sabotage the Cactus Marathon itself."

"I guess it's possible," Frank said, sounding dubious.

Nancy shook her head. "No, it can't be. Dr. Stone said that Tasio has been getting threatening letters, and a boulder that size could have killed him."

"Exactly," Frank said grimly. "It looks like someone's trying to commit murder."

Chapter

Four

AFTER A SPEEDING RIDE in the back of the ambulance, Joe arrived with Cory Weston at the hospital. It was a large coral-colored concrete building with large glass windows, parking ramps, and even a helicopter pad. The emergency room was crowded with other runners, most of them suffering from heat exhaustion.

"So where are your friends, or your folks?" Joe asked while they waited in a small examination room. "Did you come to the marathon alone?"

"Alone," Cory repeated. "That's one way of putting it."

Joe was taken aback at the bitterness in Cory's voice. Before Joe could say anything, however, the doctor arrived. She examined the injury, gently twisting and tugging, and ordered X-rays. She left, and almost immediately an orderly came to wheel Cory to the radiology lab. Joe waited twenty minutes, until the same orderly brought Cory back.

Finally alone again, Joe asked, "You said you came here alone?"

"Yeah, drove here in my pickup. No one knows I'm here. My dad doesn't want me to run marathons."

"Doesn't want you to?" Joe repeated, incredulous. Most fathers would be proud to have a son run in a marathon. And Cory was a superb runner.

"I'm a Weston," Cory said. "Westons don't do things in public unless they do it with limousines, the mayor, and half the city council. My dad always says it's good for business. I guess he means making contacts and stuff. But I don't care about that. So I left the ranch early this morning and drove up for the marathon. I left a message that I'd be back tonight, but no one knows where I went. Except Rita."

"Rita?" Joe asked.

"The housekeeper's daughter," Cory explained.

Joe's eyes lit up. "She sounds interesting."

Cory laughed. "Rita is beautiful, but she's like my sister. Her mother, Ruby, has been our housekeeper since my mother died, when I was a baby.

Rita and I grew up together. We're the same age—eighteen."

"So, hey, if you're that rich, why didn't you just bring along bodyguards?" Joe asked, joking.

Cory gave him a rueful smile. "Don't laugh. My father and my brother always have bodyguards, and usually I do, too. My dad's paranoid. He says we've all been threatened, but I've never seen any proof. I think it's all an excuse so he can watch every move we make. So sometimes I have to give them all the slip."

Joe looked seriously at Cory. "But maybe someone really *was* after you this afternoon."

"No way," Cory hooted. "First, I think my father's totally paranoid. I mean, there are so many other rich people in the world, why would someone pick on my family? Or me? And second, except for Rita, no one knew I was coming here. Absolutely no one."

"You could have been followed," Joe pointed out.

"Oh, come on," Cory scoffed. "That means they would've been following me from the moment I left the ranch. I'm sure I would have noticed."

Joe nodded. "You have a point there."

Cory grinned. "It was a total accident," he said with confidence. "Now tell me all about George."

Joe laughed, and several mischievous thoughts

crossed his mind about what to tell Cory. Joe and George had the kind of friendship where Joe teased her constantly and George always acted as if she were exasperated with him, but their little game only hid a deep and loyal friendship. He was still wondering what to reply when the door to the examination room opened.

The doctor came in, gingerly holding several X-rays. She set them against a fluorescent light board on the nearby counter.

The doctor pointed to the skeletal outline of Cory's foot on the X-ray. "You have a hairline fracture here," she said.

Cory wrinkled his brow and stared at Joe as if asking for a translation.

"A hairline fracture means the bone is cracked but not broken, isn't that right?" Joe asked. "So at least he won't need a cast."

The doctor smiled. "That's correct."

Joe turned to Cory. "I learned this stuff while training for track and field last spring."

"What about the gash above my anklebone?" Cory asked.

"You'll need a few stitches," the doctor said. "But it's nothing serious. All in all, it could have been a lot worse. But it doesn't mean you can go off running around right away, either," the doctor added. "Even hairline fractures take time to heal. You also have a sprained ankle, so you'll have to stay off your foot for at least a week."

"A week!" Cory exclaimed with dismay. "But how'll I get around—"

A knock on the door was followed immediately by the entry of a nurse with a pair of crutches.

The doctor looked at Cory. "That's how," she answered simply.

After their discoveries on the rim of the canyon, Nancy and Frank returned to where they were staying, a bed-and-breakfast ranch in the foothills north of Tucson, to wait for Joe to return from the hospital and George from the marathon. Nancy and George were in a small guest cabin, and Frank and Joe were sharing a similar cabin on the other side of a courtyard.

Waiting in Nancy's cabin seemed unbearable, until Nancy realized why. Not only couldn't they be sure the target was Cory or Tasio, but no one knew when, or even if, there would be another attempt. The shrill ring of the telephone broke the tense silence. Frank was sitting on the bed, right next to it.

"I'll get it," he said, lifting the receiver. His eyes lit up when he heard the voice. "It's Joe!"

Just then there was a loud knock on the door. As Nancy moved to answer it, the door opened. George walked in, grinning happily, with Tasio, Dr. Stone, and the other Tarahumara runners behind her. Tasio was carrying a large burlap bag.

Nancy noticed that the Indians had changed

out of their running clothes into colorful, loose-fitting shirts and shorts. Instead of bare feet, they wore sandals with thick rubber soles.

"I finished the race. My time in the Cactus Marathon was three hours and twenty-two minutes," George said, throwing her arms around Nancy in a victorious hug. "Not bad considering everything that happened."

"And my time was the same," Tasio said, smiling warmly at Nancy.

"All of our times!" Chacho shouted with a happy smile. He seemed to be the most exuberant and outgoing of the Tarahumaras, Nancy thought.

George threw an arm around Tasio's shoulders in a comradely fashion. "We crossed the finish line side by side," she said proudly.

"If the marathon had been twice as long," the runner named Celedonio said, "we could have made up for the lost time and been first to finish."

"Tasio is going to be the next Indian Olympic hero," Dr. Stone said, gazing at the young Tarahumara like a proud father. "And when he wins the gold medal, he'll use his celebrity status to fight for the survival of his people. Isn't that right, Tasio?"

Tasio flashed a shy smile and gave a slow, exaggerated shrug. "Whatever you say, Bing."

Dr. Stone clearly was not going to be put off.

"Logging companies are destroying the Tarahumara forest and causing terrible erosion," he explained. "Tasio has helped organize his people to protest against the logging interests. He even took one of the logging company owners to court."

Tasio changed the subject. "Where is Cory?"

"He and Joe are leaving the hospital now," Frank called out, hanging up the telephone. "Cory's foot will be fine. Except he's on crutches for a week."

"Dr. Stone, you remember Frank Hardy," Nancy said, reintroducing her friend.

"Do you travel to Tarahumara country a lot?" Frank asked Dr. Stone.

Dr. Stone nodded. "Yes, it's in the Sierra Madre, a mountain chain that runs down the center of northern Mexico. The Tarahumaras live in the Copper Canyon region. It's one of the most remote and beautiful areas on earth. Actually, it includes five separate canyons, and one of them is deeper than the Grand Canyon."

"Wow! I'd love to visit there sometime," Frank said.

"Well, now's your chance," Dr. Stone said. "I'm inviting Nancy and George to join me when I accompany the Tarahumara runners back to their village. You and your brother are welcome, too."

Noticing Nancy's astonishment at the invitation, Dr. Stone informed her, "I talked to your father about it when he called. Carson told me it's fine with him. In fact, he said he hoped you'd go."

Nancy checked with George and Frank.

"I'd love to," George said quickly. "Let's do it."

"But how will we get there?" Nancy asked. "Can we take our rental car to Mexico? And we didn't bring our passports."

Dr. Stone shook his head. "American citizens don't need passports to go to Mexico, as long as you have a driver's license or some other piece of identification. We'll take the night train to the Mexican city of Chihuahua and arrive tomorrow in the afternoon, then rest up overnight. On Tuesday morning we'll take the Chihuahua Pacifico train right through the Copper Canyon to a Tarahumara village called Batophilas, where Tasio and his friends live. You'll be able to see the Copper Canyon region in total comfort. People come from all over the world just to ride on that train because the scenery is so spectacular."

"I'm intrigued," Nancy confessed. "What about you?" she asked Frank.

"It sounds great," Frank answered. "But I'll have to talk to Joe first."

The conversation turned to other topics. About fifteen minutes later the door burst open and Joe walked in. Slowly walking on crutches behind him was Cory, his left foot wrapped in an elastic bandage. He held it several inches above the floor.

"Greetings, fellow runners," Joe said, making a grand gesture toward Cory. "Get him to another twenty-six-mile marathon! He wants to see what his time is on crutches."

Cory smiled sheepishly. "It's not serious, folks," he assured everyone. "Just a hairline fracture and a sprained ankle."

"Where'd all that blood on your shoe come from?" Nancy asked.

"The rock gashed my leg just above the ankle," Cory said, "and I had to have some stitches. No big deal. The worst part is, I have to limp around on crutches for about a week."

"Hey, guys," Joe said. "Cory's invited us to his dad's ranch for a few days. It's only a two-hour drive from here, and it sounds great. Horseback riding, swimming pool, tennis court, and a whole bunkhouse of cowboys to take care of us."

"Actually," Nancy said, "Dr. Stone has invited all of us to go with him to Tarahumara country. He's leaving late tonight."

Before Frank or Joe could answer, Tasio stepped forward. He reached inside the burlap sack he was carrying and took out a beautiful drum made of animal skin with a star-shaped design painted in red and black on the stretched surface.

"I can never repay you for saving my life,"

Tasio told Cory. "But I have made this with my own hands, and while I was making it, I put many prayers for good luck into it. I want you to have it, so you know I will always remember that you saved my life."

Nancy was moved by Tasio's gesture, and she noticed everyone else was, too. The room had fallen completely silent.

Cory took the drum from Tasio. "I—I don't know what to say," he stammered. "Tasio, when I saw that rock coming down on you, I just did what anyone would have."

Frank glanced at Nancy. "Should we tell them now?"

Nancy nodded. Quickly, Frank explained what they had found at the top of the canyon wall. "So it looks like that rock didn't fall by accident," he concluded. "And maybe that car at the starting line wasn't an accident, either."

"Frank and I talked about going to the police, as soon as you guys got back," Nancy said.

Bingham Stone's face had turned beet red while Nancy and Frank talked. "They were after Tasio," he said angrily. "They're trying to kill him."

"But why?" Nancy asked. "And who would do it?"

"Many of the Tarahumaras think Tasio will be a great leader someday. He was educated at a Jesuit school in the town of Creel and knows our world just as well as he knows his own. As I mentioned, he's already organized his people against the logging interests and taken them to court. The Tarahumaras lost, but they'll try again, and Tasio will lead the way. That's why people are trying to stop him."

"Do you have proof?" Joe asked. "Or is this just something you suspect?"

"Proof!" Bingham Stone boomed. He opened his canvas shoulder bag and pulled out a sheaf of folded papers. "Letters!" he said, brandishing them aloft. He rubbed one between his forefinger and thumb. "Written on very expensive paper, too. But these are death threats against Tasio Humada. If that isn't proof, I don't know what is!"

As Dr. Stone went on, Frank saw Cory turn pale and wobble on his crutches. Then his eyes rolled up into his head and he crumpled to the floor.

Chapter

Five

GEORGE INSTANTLY KNELT next to Cory. "Quick! Get a washcloth with cool water," she called out. She felt his pulse and was relieved to find it was strong and steady. Then she looked up at the Hardys. "Can you put him on one of the beds?" she asked. As Frank and Joe were lifting Cory onto a bed, he regained consciousness. Still, his face was as white as a sheet. George took the cool washcloth Nancy handed her and gently placed it on his forehead.

"Guess it all just got to me," he said. "Running almost twenty-six miles and then getting hit by a rock." Cory smiled up at George. "With a nurse like this, I'll be better soon," he said.

George blushed.

Nancy turned to her father's friend. "Dr.

Stone, George and I will have to talk about your offer. Can we have a couple of hours to think it over?"

"Absolutely," Stone said. "I'm taking the runners back to my home to rest up. The train leaves at eleven tonight. So you have until then."

"Can I look over those letters?" Nancy asked.

He hesitated a moment, then said, "Of course. Your father has told me about the cases you've solved." He handed her the letters. "But be careful with them," he went on, his tone stern. "They're important evidence."

Bingham Stone left with Tasio and the other Tarahumara runners. The room was suddenly silent. Frank, Joe, George, and Nancy looked at one another. Cory seemed to have nodded off. Joe motioned the others to step outside, to the garden.

"Seems like we have competing invitations," Frank said when they were out of Cory's earshot. "If we went with Stone and the Tarahumaras, we could all keep an eye on Tasio. And maybe stop another attempt on his life."

"Yeah, maybe, but get this," Joe interrupted. "There's some problem in Cory's family. He usually never goes anywhere without body-guards." Joe repeated what he had learned from Cory.

"Dr. Stone recognized Cory Weston's surname when I introduced them," Nancy said. "I wonder

45

why his family has to be protected by body-guards."

"Lots of money," said Joe. "Nowadays, that's enough to be well known. And maybe his dad has made some enemies along the way."

"So we're back to square one," Frank said. "Either Tasio or Cory could've been the target."

"But Cory hasn't been getting threatening letters, and Tasio has," Nancy said, holding them out.

There were six of them. Words had been clipped from magazine pages and pasted unevenly on expensive, light beige notepaper to form messages.

"None of them is signed," Nancy noted.

"'Tasio Humada,'" Frank read from the letter on top. "'Y-O-R'—that would be *You're*—'marked for death, and them other Indians is, too.'" He looked up. "Whoever sent this speaks really poor English."

"The writer can't spell, either," Nancy said.

She flipped through the other letters, with George glancing at them over her shoulder. "These are disgusting!" George exclaimed. "They're filled with swear words and racist remarks."

Joe took one of the letters and held it up to the sky. Like all expensive linen stationery, it had a watermark. "Shieldcrest," Joe said, squinting to read the faint brand name scrolled in an elaborate watermark. He handed the letter back to Nancy.

"Isn't it weird for someone who's sending death threats to use paper that's so easily identifiable?" George asked.

Nancy shrugged. "I guess the writer didn't think of that."

"Well, I think our next step is obvious," Joe said. "Frank and I will accept Cory's invitation to his ranch for a few days. You two go see Copper Canyon with Dr. Stone."

"It's perfect," George said. "We can keep our eyes on both of them—"

"And stay constantly in touch," Frank cautioned. "You guys will have to telephone us at the Weston ranch when you get to Chihuahua tomorrow night."

"We can't just let this go by without doing something," Nancy agreed. "If those threats are real, or whoever was out there today tries again, either Tasio or Cory could be killed."

Sunday evening, while Nancy and George packed for the train trip to Chihuahua, Frank and Joe left Tucson, driving Cory's white half-ton pickup. Frank drove, and Joe sat in the passenger seat. Cory sat sideways on the long, single seat behind them, with his injured leg straight out in front of him.

Following Cory's directions, Frank drove

southeast on the interstate and then turned south at the town of Benson. The highway climbed slowly upward. The sky blazed with stars, despite the steel white light of the almost full moon rising on the horizon.

In the bright, silvery moonlight, Frank could watch the vegetation change from cactus desert to grass. After driving up a long uphill grade, he saw oak trees, small and twisted, dotting the rocky hills around them. A mile later pine trees were interspersed with oaks, but the stands of trees were few and far between.

"Some of the best rangeland in the West," Cory said from the backseat. "The Double W has twenty thousand head."

"Is that the name of your ranch?" Joe asked. "The Double W?"

"Yep," Cory said. "Most people just call it the Double Double now. My dad and brother and I call it the Double Trouble when we're joking around. It's a lot of work keeping the place in shape."

"I thought you had a bunkhouse full of cowboys," Joe said.

Cory laughed. "They're in charge of the cattle, Joe. I mean, around the houses and all the various buildings."

"Houses?" Frank said. "You have more than one?"

Cory nodded. "Twenty-five years ago my dad built a big, new one. That's the house I grew up in. But the old adobe hacienda that my great-great-grandfather built is still standing, and I have it all to myself. You guys can stay with me."

"Wow, an adobe house. Sounds neat," Joe said. "Even if it is built of mud."

"Well, for mud, it's actually pretty elegant," Cory said. "A little run-down, but—well, you'll see."

"You said your great-great-grandfather built it," Frank reiterated. "I guess your family's been in Arizona a long time."

"Willis Weston was my great-great-grand-father," Cory said proudly. "He's better known in Arizona history as Willie Weston."

"Double W," Joe said. "I get it."

Cory smiled and nodded. "He was a tracker with Kit Carson and came to Arizona the same year it became American territory, when the Spanish garrisons pulled out. He fell in love with a Mexican woman who had fled the civil war south of the border, but her mother and father wouldn't let him marry her until he promised to build her a big hacienda just like the one she grew up in in Mexico. He did, and she was my great-great-grandmother."

They left the state highway and turned onto a narrow, two-lane paved road that laced up and down the rolling hills. As the road came out of a dip, Joe saw an immense, dark blotch spreading across the range.

"There's our herd," Cory announced.

Joe peered through the windshield, his eyes picking out the shapes of cattle in the moonlit darkness. "There must be thousands of them."

"Tens of thousands," Cory corrected. "The Double W is one of the largest cattle ranches in the country."

They were still driving in what Joe thought was the middle of nowhere when Cory told Frank to downshift and watch for a gate on the left side of the road.

"Right up there," Cory said, pointing from the backseat.

"Where?" Frank asked. Suddenly he saw a gate breaking the long length of barbed-wire fence that ran ten yards from the side of the highway. Dark wooden posts formed an upside-down U over the gate. Past it, a dirt road led across the range.

Frank turned and braked to an abrupt halt in front of the wide, metal gate, on which was a large No Trespassing sign. Joe jumped out and opened the gate. For someone who says his father has bodyguards, Joe thought, there's no security here at all.

Frank continued along the gravel road. It

dipped into deep hollows, where the moon
barely penetrated, and rose along the side
rolling hills. They passed more cattle, tiny, b
silhouettes dotting the side of a mountain.

"So, you ride herd on these cattle,"
drawled, in his best cowboy imitation, "acr
the barren prairie, through blinding snowstor
battling off rustlers and all that stuff."

Cory laughed. "It's a little more modern nov
days. The Santa Fe Railroad runs along the ed
of our property. We have our own private sidi
for loading cattle. The train takes them straig
to market in Kansas City."

The road began to climb again, with sha
turns taking them back and forth along the si
of a mountain. At the crest of a long slope, Fra
and Joe suddenly had a clear view of the vall
far below, where bright lights glittered. Fra
noticed a black slash cutting the land, lit by
single light. It was straight as an arrow, a
several small airplanes were parked at one en
Not far from the landing strip, a series of larg
square, windowless structures were brightly lit
outdoor halogen floodlights. A railroad tra
plowed across the valley floor like a long zipper.

"You have a private airport, too?" Frank
asked.

"Sure. We use airplanes more than cowboys on
horseback to track cattle nowadays. The pilots

can spot sick or lost animals, and then we send a Jeep out. And when you live in a backwater like this, air travel comes in handy, you know, for getting around."

"And what's that other building down there?" Joe asked. "The one with all the lights around it?"

"That's the lumber mill," Cory explained. "Dad built it twenty years ago. At first it made a lot of money, but it's fallen on hard times lately. Dad's even talking about closing it down."

"Where do you get the trees from?" Joe asked.

"That's always a problem," Cory told him. "There are huge pine forests at high elevations in the mountains, and it used to be we could get what we needed. But most of that land has been declared state forest now, and we can't get the logging permits anymore. We've had to bring in logs from farther and farther away, and it gets more and more expensive."

They were driving steadily along the summit of the mountain. Ahead, Frank noticed that the sky was lit up by bright halogen lights.

"There's a lot of candlepower up there," he noted. "Why all the bright lights?"

"That's the Double W homestead," Cory said.

The road swung around a cluster of stunted oaks, and suddenly before them a great house rose on the promontory, like a southern planta-

tion house transplanted to a landscape of oak scrub, cactus, and tall grass. The valley spread out behind it, with lights from the mill and the airstrip sparkling like tiny diamonds.

Powerful spotlights illuminated the front of the house, and Frank and Joe noticed several men sitting on the porch that ran along the front of the house. One wore a suit with a dark shirt. The other two were dressed casually in jeans and nylon jackets and carried rifles. The three men quickly stood up as the white pickup truck pulled into the long circular driveway and stopped in front of the house.

Cory waved from the back window of the king-size cab. Joe saw the two armed men relax, but the man in the suit hurried down the steps toward the truck.

"So you really do have your own private police force," Joe commented.

"I told you my dad was paranoid," Cory said half jokingly. Then he shrugged. "But maybe not. We live way out here, and people know he's rich. You never know when someone's going to try something."

Frank nodded. "It's better to be safe than sorry. There are a lot more kidnappings for ransom than people think. It's just that usually they're local events, so people only hear about the ones that happen in their own hometowns."

"You know, that's exactly what my dad says." Cory smiled. He stuck his head out the window and shouted to the man in the suit. "Hey, Sam!"

"Where have you been?" the man named Sam demanded, approaching the truck. "Your father was about ready to call in the FBI and half the private detectives in the country!"

"I left a message that I'd be back tonight," Cory said. "Didn't he get it?"

The guard nodded. "Sure he did. But you know he doesn't like you leaving here alone. Your dad was fit to be tied. It makes me look bad, with you taking off like that and not telling anyone!"

Cory sighed. "I guess I'd better go in and talk to him."

"Far as I know, everyone's asleep," Sam said. "'Cept Dick, and who knows what he's up to." He caught the eyes of the other two guards and snickered.

Cory nodded. "I want you to meet my friends, Frank and Joe Hardy. They'll be staying with me for a few days. We'll be over in the morning for breakfast."

Sam stood at the side window of the truck, peering inside at Frank and Joe, then at Cory. "What are them crutches for? You hurt yourself?" he demanded.

"Nothing serious," Cory said. "I ran in the Cactus Marathon in Tucson and ended up with a sprain and a hairline fracture."

Sam shook his head. "I'm going to be in big trouble when your dad sees that. He'll think I'm not doing my job."

"Don't worry," Cory assured Sam. "I'll tell him that I take full responsibility for leaving."

"Much obliged to you," Sam said, backing away from the truck and waving them on.

Cory directed Frank to drive ahead and take a narrower road that led between walls of prickly pear cactus and ocotillo. A grove of twisted oaks leaning over the road gave way to an adobe house, with cracked walls and antique wooden supports around the windows and doors. The house was long, with additional wings on either side enclosing a courtyard. A veranda with thick, round columns holding up a red tile roof ran along the central part of the house.

"Wow!" Joe exclaimed, stepping out of the truck. "What a place." He turned back, took out the crutches, and helped Cory down from the cab.

"Welcome to the real Double W ranch house," Cory said, leading them inside.

The interior was cool and dark, but Cory flicked a switch, and warm, soft light filled the room, glowing on stone floors that had been burnished a deep blue. The ceilings were high, and the room was filled with overstuffed sofas and worn Indian rugs in red and black geometric patterns. An enormous beehive stucco fireplace with a mantel of thick wood took up one wall. Thick tree trunks, skinned of their bark and polished, had been used as ceiling beams.

"My fortress," Cory proclaimed, dropping his crutches and collapsing on one of the sofas. "No one ever comes here."

"When was this place built?" Frank asked, setting his valise down.

"Just after the Civil War," Cory told him. "Willie Weston hired cashiered Confederate soldiers as carpenters. It was built in less than a month. Most of the soldiers left, but one stayed to hand-carve all the doors and the beams."

Cory showed them to a large bedroom in which there were twin beds with high headboards of dark polished wood. Two long windows, shaded by the boughs of a vine, opened out onto the courtyard.

"My room is across the courtyard," he told them. "See you in the morning."

After Cory left, Joe opened one of the windows and stared out into the night.

"What's the matter?" Frank asked, lying down on one of the beds. He was exhausted.

"I was just thinking that Nancy and George are on the train to Chihuahua now." He sat in a chair next to a small desk and idly pulled out the top drawer. A box of writing paper lay inside, with a stainless steel fountain pen beside it. Joe picked up the top piece of paper and rubbed it between his fingers.

"Very expensive paper," Joe said, consciously repeating Bingham Stone's words about the threatening letters that had been sent to Tasio. Then Joe held it up to the light. Instantly, he saw the faint outlines of the watermark.

"What's the watermark?" Frank asked, sitting up.

Joe lowered the paper, stunned. "Shieldcrest," he said. "It's exactly the same as the paper those death threats to Tasio were written on."

Chapter

Six

ON MONDAY MORNING Joe sat outside in the courtyard on a small stone bench near a fountain. The early morning desert air smelled sweet and held just a hint of dew before the sun's hot rays vaporized it. He couldn't stop thinking about the discovery of the letter paper the night before.

He knew that it could be a coincidence. Any number of people could have the same paper, in the same color. But Cory's behavior had been strange when he met Dr. Stone and the Tarahumaras. Could Cory be sending the letters? But why?

Joe started to worry about Nancy and George, traveling with the Tarahumaras and

Bingham Stone. If someone *was* out to kill Tasio, Nancy and George could be in terrible danger as well. They were to arrive in Chihuahua that afternoon. It would be an anxious wait, he thought, until Nancy telephoned them.

At that moment a slim, olive-skinned girl with dark eyes and waist-length, shiny black hair walked into view on the road that led to the vine-covered hacienda. She was wearing form-fitting jeans and a scooped-neck white blouse, cinched at her waist with a silver-studded, black leather belt, which emphasized her tiny waist. Joe was taken aback. He was certain he hadn't seen a more beautiful girl in his life.

"Hello, I'm Rita," she said, giving Joe a warm smile.

"I'm Joe Hardy." He stood up. "Cory told me all about you."

"Only good things, I hope," Rita said.

"Not a chance!" Cory joked, hobbling out of the house on his crutches. Frank followed him. "Only the sordid details. Joe, are you ready for breakfast at the big house?"

"That's just what I came over to tell you," Rita said. "Breakfast is waiting. My mother has been in the kitchen since dawn making all your favorite things, Cory. She thinks it will heal your leg faster."

"How'd she know about my leg?" Cory asked.

Rita smiled coyly. "Sam told us this morning that you'd come back with a couple of friends and an injured leg."

Cory ushered the Hardys into the opulent two-story foyer of the nearby mansion, where red velvet draperies hung at the tall front windows.

They were barely inside when a short, plump woman with burnished black hair worn in a bun marched through a paneled door. She wore a dark mauve dress and a white apron. "Cory, *mi querido,*" she cried, opening her arms and going straight to him. She hugged him and his crutches tightly.

"I'm okay, Tia Ruby," Cory said, finally pulling away from her and hobbling back on his crutches. "These are my friends, Frank and Joe," he announced. To the Hardys, he explained, "Ruby is our housekeeper. And my surrogate mother, sort of. That's why I call her *Tia*—Aunt —Ruby."

The housekeeper shook her finger at Cory. "That is not true. A mother does not let a son go off to run in marathons without telling anyone," she scolded.

Cory ignored her lecture. Changing the subject, he said, "Frank and Joe are detectives. When I got hit by that rock yesterday, they were ready to start an investigation."

"Into what?" a thin, sharp voice asked.

Frank and Joe turned and saw a man in his twenties walk into the room. He had blue eyes and was incredibly thin. His cowboy boots made him seem taller than he was. His eyes took in Cory's crutches and bandaged foot, but he said nothing. Rita looked away and was suddenly quiet.

"My older brother, Dick," Cory said quietly, making no further effort at introductions.

Instead of greeting them, Dick Weston repeated his question, his tone belligerent. "What were you ready to start investigating?"

To Frank it sounded more like a challenge than a question. "Nothing really," Frank said. "We think it's possible someone deliberately pushed a boulder off a cliff a half mile from the finish line. Whoever they were aiming for—it hit Cory."

"Yeah, I heard you were on crutches," Dick said. "Are you okay?"

"I'm fine," Cory said. "No big deal."

There was a long silence, and Frank stepped forward, deciding to introduce himself. "I'm Frank Hardy," he said.

"I know that, too," Dick said coldly. His blue eyes flashed at Joe. "And you're Joe Hardy. Sam told me everything." He started across the elegant foyer. Just as he got to the front door, Dick turned back to Cory. "Oh, yeah. Dad's on the patio. He wants to see you after breakfast." With that, he opened the front door and slammed it behind him.

"He's a little antisocial," Cory said apologetically.

"Antisocial?" Rita said in a low voice. "He's more like homicidal."

"Tsk," Ruby said loudly, "you children stop it." She fluttered her hands at Rita, clearly trying to stop her from saying anything more. "You boys go into the dining room," Ruby said, "before your breakfast gets cold."

"I promise you'll eat well while you're here," Cory said.

"I have to exercise my horse," Rita announced, heading for the front door. She opened it, then paused and turned back to Joe, her dark eyes glinting. "Maybe you'd like to go riding later," she suggested.

"Definitely," Joe answered quickly.

Cory led Frank and Joe through the house, which seemed to have an endless number of living rooms filled with plush couches and chairs. In the dining room Ruby served hearty platefuls of bacon, eggs, home-fried potatoes, and toast. Afterward, Cory led them to the patio behind the house. Sliding glass doors led out to a wide terrace, where a swimming pool sparkled at the edge of the promontory. The land fell away beyond it, affording a breathtaking view of the valley and the next range of mountains. An older man with snow white hair and a wide, welcoming grin sat in a chair beside a glass table.

"Call me Uncle Marcus," the man prompted when Cory introduced him to the Hardys. "Everyone else does. Guess it's because I like them to say 'uncle,'" he chortled.

Just then Dick Weston returned, stepping onto the terrace from the side of the house. He eyed the Hardys as he approached. When he was close, he broke into a smile.

"Sorry I didn't hang around inside," he said, extending his hand in a welcoming shake with both the Hardys. "I was in a hurry." He looked at Joe, then at Frank, and his smile faded. "So you think someone tried to murder Cory yesterday."

"Aw, come on, guys," Cory protested. "It was an accident."

"Accident or not, Cory, it's why I don't like you going off by yourself without taking Sam or Ernie or one of the other men with you," Marcus Weston reprimanded. Then he lowered his voice. "You don't know how dangerous it is out there. If you wanted to run the Cactus Marathon, son, I would have made sure of it. But with protection. With protection."

"Mr. Weston—" Joe started.

Cory's father quickly interrupted. *"Uncle* Marcus," he insisted.

"Okay, Uncle Marcus," Joe said, although he felt uncomfortable addressing Mr. Weston in such a way. "We *do* have reason to believe it might not have been an accident."

"Is that right?" Marcus Weston exclaimed, but didn't question Joe. "Well, you two keep right on poking your noses into this business, and I can promise you a substantial fee if you find the culprit who wanted to hurt my son."

Cory quickly changed the subject. "Frank and Joe are staying with me," he said. "I thought they'd like it better than the big house."

Addressing Frank and Joe, Mr. Weston bellowed, "You want to stay out in that drafty old place?" He shook his head. "I was going to rip it down last year. Put in a nine-hole golf course—until Cory got it into his head to live in it.

"I tried to tell him nothing lasts forever. You got to get on with living, and bring on the future. Now, take that mill down there," he said, pointing down into the valley. "We can't get logs for it because all the pine trees within a hundred miles are called state forest. I'm going to have to close that mill down if I can't get logs."

"But, Dad, we found a way to get logs," Dick protested.

"We *hope* we have," Marcus Weston said. "What with this free-trade zone between us and the Mexicans, there'll be lots of changes coming. Maybe enough logs for our mill, too."

"I was going to take Frank and Joe out riding," Cory said. Joe thought he seemed anxious to get away.

Marcus Weston told Frank and Joe to enjoy the ranch and promised to see them again at lunch.

Cory, who was getting fast on his crutches, led the Hardys out to a long horse barn attached to corrals and roofed stables. As they approached, Joe saw Rita riding a black and white Appaloosa at a brisk trot in wide circles, her black hair flying behind her. Seeing them, Rita waved and reined her horse in.

"I'll wait for you out here," she called.

An old wrangler met them at the door of the stable and helped the Hardys select horses. Joe took to a sandy gelding almost immediately.

The wrangler shrugged. "This one's got pepper in 'im," he said grimly. "That's 'is name, Pepper."

"I can handle him," Joe said confidently. He took the reins and quickly mounted. Pepper lurched, snorted, and twisted his neck. Joe dug his heels into the horse's flanks and held on firmly to the reins. Pepper quickly settled down, and Joe trotted out into the corral in search of Rita.

Frank chose a black gelding, while Cory rode a beautiful chestnut brown stallion with a long white streak on his muzzle. With the help of the wrangler, Cory managed to mount the horse.

"Are you sure you can manage with the bum foot?" Frank asked.

"No sweat," Cory assured him. "I need it for walking, not riding."

The wrangler held open the gate, and the four of them rode out. Cory led them on a winding gravel road along the side of the mountain. "There's an old ghost town up here," he told them.

Soon the road was nothing more than a narrow path of broken stones winding among twisting oaks, tall yellow grass, and spiky yuccas. It twisted into a deep ravine, and almost immediately Frank spotted the ruins of an old stone building. Soon there was another, then a few wooden shacks, with light visible through cracks in the siding. Most of the roofs had caved in. A wooden sidewalk that had once run along the front of the buildings had collapsed into a long thread of shattered, weathered wood.

As they rode farther along the trail, Joe noticed that there were gaping holes in the cliffs. "That's what's left of the silver mine," Cory explained. "The vein lasted about eight years. When it ran out, my grandfather bought the whole town."

"The Westons like to own things," Rita said in a mocking tone.

Cory scowled. "There's nothing wrong with owning things."

Frank and Joe wondered if they had stumbled into a family argument. "Let's ride ahead," Frank suggested.

"Okay by me," Joe replied.

Frank saw a row of oak trees and beyond them open sky, where the land broke at a precipice. He dug his heels into his horse's flanks, urging it to move faster. The horse galloped toward the trees.

"Yahoo!" Joe shouted, following right behind.

They both pulled up ten feet short of the edge of the cliff. Below, they saw the valley with the airstrip running down its center.

Frank heard a distant buzzing sound. At the far end of the valley, he spotted an airplane heading toward the airstrip. Instead of veering across the valley, however, the pilot maintained a line along the side of the mountain. Being a pilot, Frank quickly determined that the airplane was traveling with a tailwind and had to approach the landing strip from the opposite direction. As the plane flew in their direction, Frank noticed that the pilot was edging the plane from side to side.

"He's trying to get a look at us," Frank called to Joe over the noise of the engines. Almost before they knew it, the airplane was several hundred feet in front of them. It was so close, Frank could see two people in the front seat of the small white plane, and a third person in the seat behind.

Joe felt Pepper tremble and shiver. Quickly, he

turned the horse away from the precipice. The horse whinnied and reared up on his hind legs.

"Whoa!" Joe shouted. He leaned forward, twisting the reins in his hands to shorten them. The horse reared again. Joe knew he was only moments away from being thrown over the cliff!

Chapter

Seven

J UST THEN the airplane swerved, turning sharply over the valley, and headed back to the airstrip.

Pepper's front hooves crashed to the ground. Frank carefully positioned his horse to keep Joe's skittish animal from getting any closer to the cliff edge. Joe, breathing a deep sigh of relief, urged Pepper back.

"Thanks," Joe said to his brother, stroking Pepper's neck.

Cory and Rita rode up then, squinting at the disappearing airplane.

"Whose plane is that?" Frank asked. "The pilot sure came close to the cliff, and Joe's horse freaked out."

For a moment Cory didn't answer. Then he

said, "Oh, just one of my dad's business partners."

Then Cory turned to Rita. "Hey, Rita," he said quickly, "let's take them down to the hot mineral springs at the bottom of Pistol Hill." Without waiting for a response, he spurred the chestnut stallion and galloped back to the oak trees, where a trail wound down the side of the mountain.

"Nice of him to wait for an answer," Joe muttered.

Rita gave the younger Hardy an apologetic smile. "He's a Weston," she said, as if that explained everything.

The day passed quickly, with lunch and a hilarious game of croquet after the meal. Then Frank and Cory took off, leaving Joe and Rita alone. They decided to have a swim in the pool beside the main house. As they approached, they heard an angry voice speaking in Spanish. Joe saw a small, thin man with dark skin and black hair standing on the patio. He was yelling at Dick and Marcus Weston. Sam and Ernie were close behind them. A car was idling in the driveway.

Rita stopped and pulled Joe behind a rose-covered arbor beside the house.

"What's that all about?" Joe murmured.

Rita shrugged. "I don't know. Probably just more Weston business. But we shouldn't interrupt."

Joe watched as the little man spoke more rapidly, and Joe noticed something glint in the man's mouth—a silver tooth. Marcus Weston nodded at Sam, and spoke.

"Get him out of here," he ordered. "I want that airplane off the grounds immediately."

The guards moved forward to shove the little man into the car. Sam slid behind the wheel, and the Westons went back inside.

"Come this way," Rita said, plucking at Joe's sleeve. Joe watched the car speed down the driveway. With a last backward glance, he let Rita lead him through the rose garden to a small pool house at the side of the patio. After changing, Joe stepped to the edge of the pool and saw the small twin-prop plane take off from the landing strip in the valley below. He noted that it was headed south. Toward Mexico? he wondered. He turned back to the pool, took a deep breath, and dove in.

Joe swam a long time, letting the water massage his sore muscles. Afterward, he lay on his stomach on a lounge chair, soaking up the rays of the hot midafternoon sun. Rita sat down beside him and started massaging his back, her small hands prodding and kneading his sore muscles with surprising strength.

"That feels good," Joe said.

"You need to relax more, Joe," Rita said. "I can feel the tension in your back."

"Mmm," Joe said. "You weren't so relaxed yourself this morning when we were riding. You and Cory acted like you were having some sort of family argument. I mean, I know you're not family exactly, but Cory said you're like a sister to him."

Rita smiled. "He said that?" She seemed pleasantly surprised. "I'm glad. At least he knows who some of his friends are."

"What does that mean?" Joe asked, rolling over to look at her. Again he was taken aback by her beauty.

Rita gave a careless shrug, but Joe saw her eyebrows furrow with concern. "Uncle Marcus is ruthless."

"What do you mean?"

Rita was silent for a long moment. Finally she spoke. "Marcus Weston wants his sons to be just like him, and Cory's not. Cory's different. Right now Marcus gives Cory some room, but sooner or later Marcus will demand his son's loyalty. And Cory will have to decide."

"Decide what?" Joe asked.

Rita sat up and grabbed her towel. "Come on, I have to go." She headed for the pool house.

After they'd changed, Joe walked Rita to a small adobe-style house a half mile off the main road, where she lived with her mother.

"I really enjoyed spending the day with you," Joe told her.

Rita smiled. She smoothed back a strand of her long black hair and moved a little closer to Joe. "It was wonderful. I hope we can spend more time together while you're here."

"Me, too," Joe answered, and bent forward to kiss Rita lightly on the lips. Rita took his hand and squeezed it. Then wordlessly she turned and went inside the little house.

Joe stood staring after her for a moment, thinking about how soft her lips had been. Then he shook his head and reminded himself why he was here. Quickly, he returned to the hacienda.

Frank was there, alone, and Joe told him about the encounter he'd witnessed at the house.

Before Frank could say anything, Cory walked in. "Dinner's in about fifteen minutes," he said. "Are you ready?"

At dinner, Frank was aware of the tension at the table. Marcus Weston was subdued, and Dick Weston ate in complete silence, not even glancing up from his plate. Only Cory seemed oblivious to the tension. He and Joe talked about their plans for future marathons.

After dinner they returned to the hacienda to crash in front of the television set.

Darkness fell, and Cory turned in. Joe gave a loud yawn and realized he was exhausted. He glanced at his watch and was surprised to see that it wasn't quite nine o'clock. He was about to go to bed when the telephone rang.

"I hope it's Nancy," Frank said, reaching for the phone. He put it to his ear and gave Joe a curt nod to confirm his guess. "They made it to Chihuahua safe and sound."

Frank and Nancy exchanged accounts of what had transpired since they left Tucson. "Something mysterious is definitely going on here," Nancy told him, relating events that had happened to her that day.

"There are some weird vibes around here, too," Frank told her. "For one thing, Joe discovered letter paper exactly the same as the kind those death threats were written on."

Nancy was stunned. "You think one of the Westons made those threats against Tasio?"

"It's only circumstantial," Frank pointed out. "And there are a lot of hired hands here, too, so it might've been any of them. Or it might just be a coincidence."

After Nancy said goodbye, Frank was about to hang up when he heard a telltale click on the line.

Someone at the Weston ranch had been eavesdropping on his telephone conversation!

Chapter
Eight

N ANCY, WAKE UP," George said, giving Nancy's shoulder a shake. "We're in Mexico now."

Nancy sat up in her berth in the sleeping car of the train and peeked out the window. The train was passing farmland, and Nancy could see cornfields. "Looks more like the Midwest to me."

"I know," George agreed. "For a few moments this morning I thought the train had gone in the wrong direction! Dr. Stone told me those farms belong to Mennonites, a religious sect that migrated here fifty years ago. Anyway," she said, standing, "hurry up. We're having breakfast in the dining car."

Nancy couldn't believe how well she had slept. She and George had met Dr. Stone and the

Tarahumara runners at the train station in Arizona the night before. Dr. Stone had already arranged for the sleeping berths, and George and Nancy had gone to bed immediately. Now it was Monday morning, and they were in Mexico!

After washing up and putting on khaki pants and a dark brown T-shirt, Nancy ran into Tasio, Chacho, and Celedonio. The porter had already tied the curtains back and folded their berths into seats. The Tarahumaras wore their traditional clothing again. Nancy was intrigued by the brightly colored baggy cotton shirts and loose-fitting white shorts.

"Your clothes look so comfortable," Nancy said.

"These are called *napatzas*," Chacho explained, pulling at the fabric of his bright blue shirt. He gave her a wide smile.

Nancy returned his smile. She liked his warmth and friendliness.

"And this is a *tagora*." Tasio pointed to what she had thought were shorts.

"Is that a single piece of cloth?" she asked.

Tasio nodded. *"Sí,* it is shaped like a triangle, and we wrap it around our hips." He pointed to a brand-new nylon pouch he wore around his waist. "I bought this in Tucson. A *tagora* doesn't have pockets, so this is very useful for carrying money and identification papers."

"Well, I love your *napatzas*," Nancy said,

carefully pronouncing the foreign word. "Maybe I will be able to buy one like it in your village."

Celedonio stared at her but said nothing. To Nancy, he seemed arrogant. But perhaps he was just shy, she thought.

Chacho's white teeth gleamed. "We will help you find them. In Chihuahua. There is a market there."

"Are you coming to eat breakfast?" Nancy asked.

The Tarahumara runners stared at one another uncertainly. Then Tasio spoke for them all. "We prefer to eat our own food," he said simply.

"Well, I'm starving. I'll see you guys later." Nancy made her way through the cars until she found the dining car, where other passengers sat at tables covered with white linen cloths. She joined Dr. Stone and George.

"Why won't Tasio and his friends eat with us?" Nancy asked when she was seated.

"Their digestive systems really can't handle western food," Dr. Stone explained. "For centuries, Native Americans here have survived on vegetables like corn and beans, and very little meat. Years ago the American government distributed free food on reservations. But instead of helping the Indians, it caused malnutrition because their bodies can't process it. So it's much better for the Tarahumaras to maintain their own diet."

"Is the city of Chihuahua where the little dogs 0came from?" George asked.

"It certainly is," Dr. Stone affirmed. "The *perritos chihuahueños* are a small local species. In fact, packs of chihuahuas used to run wild in the streets."

George made a face. "Can you imagine walking downtown with packs of wild chihuahuas nipping at your heels?" she said.

"Not a pleasant thought," Nancy agreed.

They arrived in the city of Chihuahua in late afternoon. As soon as Nancy and George stepped from the old railroad terminal, the pleasant energy of a Mexican city surrounded them. The sidewalks were jammed with shoppers who pushed in and out of the open-front stores that lined the streets.

Bingham Stone flagged two taxis to take the group to the hotel, and soon they were driving down an elegant, wide boulevard where fountains splashed beneath tall rows of palm trees. The taxis turned into an older part of the city, where the streets were narrow, and finally arrived at a wide wooden gate set in a high adobe wall. The doors swung back, and the taxis entered a Spanish-style courtyard, where a three-tiered fountain spun rivulets of water into cascading bowls.

The innkeeper, a jovial, plump man named Señor Rodriguez, led the party to their rooms on the second floor, where a wide, covered veranda, shaped like a U, faced the courtyard. The wooden columns holding up the roof were blanketed in pink bougainvillea blossoms.

"The train leaves in the morning at eight," Dr. Stone told Nancy and George before they went into the room they were sharing. "But while you're here, you should explore the old part of the city. The cathedral and governor's palace are fantastic. According to local legend, they are linked by underground tunnels."

Nancy and George's room had a tiny bathroom and twin beds. Double French doors led out onto the wide veranda, and from there they could look down over the courtyard.

"It's enchanting," Nancy proclaimed after they'd washed up and were ready to explore.

George held her 35mm camera and snapped a picture of the courtyard. "I just put in a new roll of film with twenty-four exposures," she said. "I figure I'll use it up in Chihuahua and start a new roll tomorrow morning on the train."

Nancy and George descended the wide, antique stairs and crossed the courtyard to the gate that led to the street. The sun beat down mercilessly on the narrow street of two-story stucco buildings. They stopped at a magazine stand and bought an English-language guidebook to the city, which included a map.

They set out for the Plaza de la Constitución,

the site of the cathedral Dr. Stone had suggested they see. They found it easily, and George immediately began photographing the beautiful baroque building from the side streets.

When George was finished taking pictures of the pink limestone structure, they walked into the square. To their surprise, they spotted Tasio and Chacho. Both Tarahumaras looked troubled. Nancy and George hurried over to them. "Tasio, Chacho, is something wrong?"

The two men were surprised to see George and Nancy. "I've been robbed," Tasio said. "A pickpocket took my new pouch."

"With all his money," Chacho said angrily.

"And my identification papers, too. It is forbidden not to carry them in Mexico." Tasio looked genuinely alarmed.

"When did this happen?" Nancy asked.

"Just a moment ago," Tasio said. "We went into the cathedral, and we were walking back across the square when a man bumped into me. I thought it was just an ordinary thing because people are always in a hurry. Something made me feel for the pouch at my waist, and it was gone. I knew immediately that this man had taken it."

"But the man had disappeared," Chacho added.

"We should report it to the police," Nancy said. "I'm sure the thief will just throw the pouch away after he takes the money. Someone might find it and turn it in to the police. At least that way, you'd get your ID papers back."

Tasio nodded in agreement. "Yes, I think we should. Besides, if we do not report it, the thief will never be caught." He paused and then added sorrowfully, "In the Barranca del Cobre, where Tarahumara people live—you call it Copper Canyon—we do not have pickpockets—yet."

The word *yet* made Nancy enormously sad. Although she'd heard only a little about the Tarahumaras' land, she knew it was remote from the modern world, and such places—and the native cultures of the people who lived there—were rapidly disappearing.

George noticed a police officer and waved him over. Tasio and Chacho launched into rapid Spanish, telling him what had happened. The officer explained something to Tasio, pulled a thick notepad and pen from the breast pocket of his uniform, and began to jot down information.

"This is Constable Martinez," Tasio told Nancy and George. "He says it is useless now because the thief has run away. We can only wait to see if someone turns in the pouch. In the meantime, I must go to a nearby police station and apply for temporary identification papers."

Martinez put away his report book and flashed his warm brown eyes at Nancy and George.

"Perhaps the thief will make a mistake the next

time, and we will catch him," he said in lightly accented English. "But, señoritas, there are many tourists who come to Chihuahua, and there are unfortunately many thieves who prey on them. I must warn you to be very cautious."

When Constable Martinez was finished, Tasio left with Chacho to go to the police station. "After I get my temporary papers, I am finished for the day," Tasio said. "I will eat and go to bed."

Nancy caught George glancing down at her camera, and knew her friend wanted to take more pictures of the old part of the city.

"But you should go inside the cathedral," Tasio urged them. "It is very beautiful."

They parted, and Nancy and George skirted traffic and pigeons as they crossed the square toward the massive cathedral.

They entered the cool silence, with dozens of candles flickering in the dim interior, and saw people in the pews, gathered for an evening mass. No priest was present at the huge gold altar, but incense burners glowed, as gray vapor drifted upward lazily.

They walked quietly to one side, careful not to disturb the worshipers. Enormous paintings of biblical scenes had been hung along the stucco walls. They were gazing at one when Nancy felt George nudge her. When she looked at her friend, George remained silent, but Nancy saw her eyes drift to the right and gaze quickly past Nancy's shoulder before turning toward the painting again.

Nancy casually glanced in the direction George had indicated. She saw a short, swarthy man in an old blue suit and white fedora standing at the cathedral door. It wasn't the first time she had seen him.

Nancy turned back to the painting again. "I saw him earlier," she whispered to George. She adjusted her position so he was within her peripheral vision, just in time to see him turn away and step outside.

"We passed him on our way across the square," Nancy whispered. "After we left Tasio and Chacho."

"That's when I first noticed him, too," George said. "He was walking across the square after us. Then I saw him staring at us from the doorway."

Nancy pointed to a side door. "If we hurry, maybe we can lose him."

They opened the thick wooden door, and Nancy cautiously peered out. Already the gloom of dusk was gathering. Flocks of birds coiled in endless winding circles over the square. Traffic had died down, and the plaza had emptied out. The man who'd been spying on them was nowhere to be seen.

They decided to return to the hotel and followed the same streets back. Nancy glanced over her shoulder and saw the man again. He was at the end of the street, intently staring at them.

"He's back," Nancy muttered. "Don't look! Pretend everything's normal, but let's move a little faster."

The street was still crowded with housewives carrying groceries home for the evening meal and children in school uniforms playing. At the end of the street, Nancy stopped as if to look in a store window. Out of the corner of her eye, she saw the man again, leaning up against a wall and waiting for them to move on.

"All the streets on the way back to the hotel should have lots of people on them," George said. "Maybe we should just keep going and call the police when we get there."

"I don't like the idea of leading him to where we're staying," Nancy said.

"I don't either," George agreed.

Nancy motioned to the street ahead, where souvenir and crafts shops lined the sidewalks and hawkers tried to sell toys and rattan mats. A crowded but shady arcade led through the block to the next street over.

"Let's try to lose him in there," she said. She knew the best strategy was to stay in a public place with lots of people.

George clutched her camera tightly to her chest, and they ran quickly through traffic, leaving a cacophony of car horns honking in their wake. They slipped into the crowd of shoppers and tourists milling through the arcade.

Suddenly the girls came to an abrupt halt at a thick wall of people, undulating to a rapid beat. A mariachi band was right in front of them, blocking their exit. Nancy saw a second arcade running sideways from where they were. It was narrower and almost empty. At the far end, glass doors led outside to another street.

"Let's go out that way," Nancy said.

George shuddered. "I hope he's not out there, waiting."

Glancing carefully around, they slipped through the crowd to the smaller arcade. They passed several hair-dressing salons and a dentist's office. A moment later they went through double doors onto a side street. A line of cars idled, waiting for a traffic light to change. A long double line of teenagers neatly dressed in school uniforms walked past, singing and chattering. Nancy oriented herself.

"This way," she decided, pointing in what she thought was the direction of the hotel. She saw George look over her shoulder and gasp. Nancy swung around.

The short, swarthy man had just turned the corner onto the side street. He came to a stop, blocked by the double line of teenagers. His eyes darted in every direction.

"Let me take his picture," George said, raising

her camera. "If he thinks we're onto him, maybe he'll run the other way."

Before Nancy could reply, the stranger turned in their direction, and George's camera shutter clicked. "I've got him!" George exclaimed.

Nancy saw a flash of anger cross the man's face. "But he's not taking off!"

The stranger clenched his fists and started toward them.

"We've got to get out of here," Nancy cried. "He's coming right for us!"

Chapter

Nine

NANCY SAW AN OPENING in the traffic. "Let's go!" she cried, grabbing George's arm and pulling her along. The two girls raced into the space between two cars just as the traffic light at the end of the street changed to green. The cars began to move forward.

They made it to the other side, then turned. Nancy saw their pursuer step into the street and then jump back, barely escaping being hit by a truck.

"This way," Nancy said.

The streets were still crowded with shoppers browsing through open-front stores. Nancy and George quickly blended in with the throng.

"There's our hotel just ahead," Nancy said.

"Thank goodness," George replied.

The door set in the wooden gates of the courtyard was open. Nancy and George quickly stepped through it, then shut it firmly behind them. They both heaved deep sighs.

Nancy instantly turned back to the door and opened the little wooden peephole at eye level. "Is he still there?" George asked.

"No," Nancy said with relief, and closed the peephole.

"I got a great snapshot of him," George said proudly.

"I'd hate to think what he might have done if he'd caught up to us," Nancy remarked. "He looked vicious. I'm sure he would have snatched your camera."

"Probably," George agreed. "Should we go to the police?"

Nancy thought for a moment. "I don't know if the police can do anything. They might not even believe us."

"So now what? Should I get this developed?" George asked.

"I don't think we're going to find a one-hour developing store in Chihuahua. Maybe we should just keep the film in a very safe place until we have time to get it developed."

As they stepped into the courtyard, Nancy heard Bingham Stone calling to them from the second-floor veranda. "Come and join us for dinner! The Tarahumaras have been to the market and prepared a feast."

Dinner with the Indian runners proved to be a real treat. Patricio and Vitorio had brought a huge basket of food to the hotel from a Chihuahua marketplace. Everyone gathered in their room.

"It's Tarahumara take-out!" George exclaimed as paper plates piled high with fresh, hot tamales were passed around. The tamales had been wrapped in corn husks and steamed. When the husks were unwrapped, the mixture of ground corn and meat inside was still piping hot. Cardboard containers of a delicious curdlike dish called *pipian* made the rounds next. Dr. Stone explained that it was made from squash seeds, boiled and ground very fine, and flavored with hot chilis.

For dessert, Celedonio passed around a basket of pine nuts and handed out plump pink fruit that Bingham Stone called cactus "tunas." By the time Nancy had sampled everything, she felt stuffed.

After everyone had eaten, Dr. Stone handed out train tickets, reminding them that the train left at exactly eight in the morning. While Celedonio and Chacho cleared away the remains of the little banquet, conversation turned to the threatening letters Tasio had received.

"They have all been sent to the post office in Batophilas, the village near my family's *ranchería,*" Tasio explained. "Except for the last one."

"And that was delivered to my home in Tucson," Dr. Stone said, "after the Tarahumaras had arrived for the marathon."

"There's a clue right there," George pointed out. "The person sending the letters must be close to Tasio because he obviously knew his schedule."

Dr. Stone shook his head. "Not necessarily. The daily newspaper did an article on the runners a few days before the marathon. It mentioned that I was their sponsor and that they were staying with me. At first the letters seemed like pranks, but then more of them came, and each was more hateful than the one before. Clearly they were written by an ignorant racist."

"And perhaps a dangerous one as well," Nancy concluded.

"It angers me that Tasio gets these letters, when his only 'crime' is to stand up for the rights of his people," Dr. Stone said.

"A very rich man named Bernardo Lupe claimed the right to cut trees on Tarahumara land," Celedonio said, joining them, anger burning in his eyes. "Tasio led our struggle to fight him. We marched to the governor's palace in

Chihuahua and blocked the highway leading to Creel, the Mexican town near our land. But in the end we lost."

That was the most Celedonio had spoken since she had met him, Nancy thought. Clearly, he was upset and angry.

Tasio continued. "We took our case to the Mexican court, where a judge found against us. But next time, perhaps we will win and be able to protect our forests."

"When the trees are cut down," Chacho explained, "the soil cannot hold water and is washed away when the snow melts. As a result, the land turns into desert."

"Bernardo Lupe and his business associates bribed the judge to decide against the Tarahumaras," Dr. Stone said. "We can't prove this, but it's the only explanation for the court's decision. And Lupe is powerful enough to do it. He has every official in the state of Chihuahua in his vest pocket."

"But if these people can buy politicians and judges, why would anyone threaten Tasio simply for leading a democratic protest?" Nancy asked.

"Bribes are expensive," Dr. Stone explained. "It is much cheaper to get rid of people who are leading protests. In Brazil, several Indian leaders have been murdered for trying to stop the destruction of the rain forests."

"And these murderers have gotten away with it because they are very rich and very powerful," Tasio said. "They make their own law, and to violate their law is to risk death."

"It's very brave of you to decide to fight for your people even when there might be great danger," Nancy said to Tasio.

He shrugged. "I have no choice. How can I not fight for the future of the Tarahumaras?"

"We have an early morning ahead of us," Dr. Stone announced, concluding his sentence with an enormous yawn. "I suggest some shut-eye."

Nancy and George returned to their room, but neither was sleepy. Nancy stood at the open French doors, breathing in the scent of the many flowers and reveling in the warm evening breeze. In River Heights, winter was fast on its way.

The courtyard and veranda were deserted, although lights glowed from several windows. Dr. Stone's and the Tarahumaras' rooms were dark.

Nancy glanced at her watch—it was almost eight o'clock. After calculating the one-hour time difference, she knew she had to telephone Frank and Joe right then. "George," she called into the room, "I promised Joe and Frank I'd call tonight. Want to go down with me to use the pay phone?" None of the rooms had phones, but there was a public one just inside the courtyard.

"Sure," George said, putting down the guide-book she'd been reading.

As they strolled along the veranda, Nancy heard loud voices arguing downstairs.

She saw Bingham Stone and Tasio engaged in conversation with a third man, a large, rotund figure dressed entirely in black. His round, red face seemed to float above his white clerical collar. Bingham Stone was gesturing angrily. Then Nancy heard the man in the clerical collar say, "You can trust him now. He has repented completely."

Bingham Stone lashed back angrily. "I refuse! I don't trust him a minute. Not until——"

Stone stopped when he noticed Nancy and George at the top of the stairs. His face was red with anger, but he forced a smile. "Well, well, what a surprise," he said as pleasantly as possible.

Nancy and George descended. The man Stone was talking with eyed them warily. He was a great bear of a man, Nancy thought. She noticed that his thick, bushy eyebrows were drawn together, and his mouth was twisted in a grimace.

Dr. Stone introduced Nancy and George to Father Sebastien, a Jesuit missionary and doctor.

"Father Sebastien came to Chihuahua from Montreal almost thirty years ago," Dr. Stone told them. "I met him through my work with the Tarahumaras." Despite the friendly lilt to his voice, Nancy sensed an underlying tension. Stone was nervous about something.

The Jesuit nodded curtly, without saying a word. He glared at the two girls, and Nancy was convinced he didn't want them to join their conversation.

"It's been very nice meeting you, Father Sebastien," Nancy said politely. "We were just about to make a phone call."

"And we are on our way upstairs," Dr. Stone said, mustering a tone of nonchalance, despite his expression. The priest glanced at Nancy and gave another curt nod.

Nancy and George moved across the courtyard. Next to the gate, a small niche held a coin-operated telephone. Nancy tried it, but it was out of order.

"Great," Nancy said, hanging up the receiver. "Care to go for a walk to find a working telephone?"

"Sure," George said. "I wouldn't mind walking off that meal. I'm still stuffed."

A few blocks from their hotel, the girls found a working pay phone. Nancy dialed the operator and gave her the number of the Double W in her schoolgirl Spanish. The operator told her it would take several minutes to place the call.

Nancy hung up the receiver and waited for the operator to call back.

"I wonder what Dr. Stone and that priest were arguing about?" George mused.

Nancy shrugged. "Beats me. I definitely had the feeling that Father Sebastien didn't want us around, though."

"Me, too," George agreed. "I know Dr. Stone is a friend of your father, but do you ever feel he's kind of strange? Like when he met Cory yesterday. He was very unfriendly."

Nancy nodded. "I noticed that, too. And he didn't want us around any more than Father Sebastien did. Mostly, Dr. Stone is really polite and friendly. But sometimes I catch glimpses of another side of him. As if he has—"

"A secret," George concluded.

"Exactly," Nancy agreed.

"Do you have any idea what it might be?"

"No," Nancy admitted. "It may have something to do with these threats against Tasio. But that's only a guess."

When the phone rang, Nancy picked it up, and through the crackle of static she heard Frank's voice.

"What's up?" George asked when the call was over and Nancy had hung up the receiver.

Nancy mentioned the notepaper that Joe had discovered.

"Do you really think someone at the Weston ranch sent those threatening letters to Tasio?"

Nancy shrugged. "It might be nothing more than a coincidence," she pointed out. "Cory had never met any of the Tarahumaras."

"But Cory didn't seem overly anxious to meet them," George pointed out.

Nancy sighed. "You're right," she said. "And Dr. Stone was pretty rude to Cory."

By the time they returned to their room, there was no sign of Dr. Stone, Tasio, or the strange priest. The girls went to bed, setting their alarm for six o'clock. Nancy slept restlessly. She dreamed of the incident during the marathon when Tasio had almost been killed. She kept seeing the boulder sliding down the side of the canyon, and felt paralyzed, unable even to scream, to warn him.

She jerked awake and lay in bed, her mind returning to Bingham Stone's strange behavior, the threatening letters, the man who had followed them through the streets of Chihuahua, and the odd, unfriendly priest in the courtyard below. Something was going on. She only wished she knew what it was.

Unable to sleep, Nancy threw back the covers, pulled on her robe over her nightshirt, and stepped outside to the veranda. The early morning air was crisp and cool, suffused with a perfumed humidity. The courtyard was still dark, but she could see the sky beginning to lighten.

Then she heard it, a noise in the courtyard below. She peered down over the railing, squinting into the semidarkness. Tasio was in the courtyard. As he walked, Nancy could see that he was sweaty. He must have been out running, she thought, although it seemed a strange time of night to exercise.

She watched him head toward the tile steps, when suddenly a light in a downstairs room came on. Shoes clicked on the tile floor inside.

Nancy saw Tasio jump into the shadows at the side of the courtyard where the old bougainvillea sprawled up the wall and branched across the posts that ran along the veranda. She could barely see him there, as a woman moved into the courtyard with a broom in hand and began sweeping.

What Nancy saw next was almost unbelievable. When the woman's back was turned to him, Tasio reached into the branches of the bougainvillea and began to climb, pulling himself up limb to limb. He climbed without making a sound. In fact, the bougainvillea barely trembled, despite his weight. Finally Tasio reached the second-floor veranda.

After he crawled over the railing, he turned, and his eyes met Nancy's straight on. He paused a moment, seeing her but not acknowledging her. Instead, he slipped across the veranda and into his room.

Clearly, Nancy thought, Tasio had not wanted to be seen.

She went back to bed, her mind riveted on a single question: What was Tasio up to?

Chapter

Ten

Nancy finally fell asleep again and awakened to the sound of a jay on the veranda outside. She could hear the sound of running water behind the bathroom door. George's bed was empty.

Nancy threw back the covers, hopped from the bed, and flung open the curtains, squinting against the sudden rush of sunlight. A quick glance at her travel alarm clock showed that it was almost six-thirty. She hadn't heard it go off! The bathroom door opened and George came out, a towel wrapped around her wet hair.

"You must have really been tired," George said. "You didn't even hear the alarm. I thought I'd let you sleep until after I had my shower." She took the towel off her head, picked up a comb, and ran it through her short, curly hair. "Dr. Stone said there'd be a continental breakfast downstairs and taxis to take us to the train station at twenty minutes to eight."

By the time Nancy showered and dressed, George's bags were neatly packed and on the bed.

"Did you see my camera?" George asked the moment Nancy walked out of the bathroom.

"Not since yesterday," Nancy told her. "Where did you put it when we got back here?"

George thought hard for a moment. "I think I just threw it on the bed and rushed out to have dinner with the Tarahumaras."

"So when you went to bed last night, did you move it?" Nancy asked.

"It wasn't there," George said slowly. "I'm sure it wasn't."

Nancy rummaged through her own suitcase and helped George search the room again. The camera was nowhere.

"It had the picture in it of the man who followed us yesterday," George pointed out.

"You mean you *left* the film in the camera?" Nancy asked.

George nodded. "I still had most of the roll left, and—" Suddenly she had a horrible realization. "He probably saw us come to the hotel, after all! Then he sneaked in and stole it." George slumped to the bed. "I really loved that camera," she said sorrowfully. "When do you think he got in here?"

Nancy thought a moment. "It could have been several different times. When we were having dinner, or maybe later, when we made that phone call to Frank and Joe."

"Should we report it to the police?" George asked.

"I'm not sure what good it will do," Nancy said, glancing at her travel alarm clock. It was a quarter after seven. "And we don't have time," she pointed out.

Nancy and George arrived in the lobby with their bags in hand and surveyed the continental breakfast—rolls and pastries, doughnuts, pitchers of fresh-squeezed orange juice, and a stainless steel urn of coffee. They helped themselves, then strolled out to the courtyard.

The Tarahumara runners were waiting, their extra clothing wrapped in white canvas, tied together with sisal.

"Bing is with you?" Tasio asked, smiling brightly when he saw Nancy and George.

Nancy remembered seeing Tasio early that morning, arriving sweaty and panting, before slipping silently up the vine and onto the veranda. For a moment she wondered if it had been a dream. Nancy shook her head. "We haven't seen him."

Tasio turned to Chacho and said something rapidly. Chacho raced into the hotel. "The taxis will be here any minute," Tasio said. "This is not like Bing. Usually he's waiting to make sure we're on time."

Tasio sounded cheerful, but Nancy thought she detected a note of worry. "In Tara country, time has another meaning altogether," he told her. "You will see."

Chacho raced from the hotel. "His room is empty," he said, clearly puzzled.

At that moment Señor Rodriguez, the innkeeper, carried several green canvas valises to the courtyard gates.

"Those are Dr. Stone's," George said.

The innkeeper appeared startled. "Yes, of course. The taxis will be here any moment, and Dr. Stone left instructions that if he was not back by morning, to make certain his luggage was delivered to the train station."

"Where did he go?" Nancy asked.

Señor Rodriguez shrugged. "He didn't tell me, señorita," he answered in a voice that told Nancy he considered it none of his business. "He left late last night in a taxi."

Nancy turned to Tasio. "Did he say anything to you about this?"

Tasio shook his head. "Something unexpected, perhaps," he said quietly.

"I'm certain Señor Stone will meet you at the station," the innkeeper said.

"He gave us our train tickets last night," George pointed out. "Maybe he had somewhere else to go this morning and forgot to tell us."

A loud honk sounded on the other side of the wooden gates. The innkeeper peered through the peephole, then reached for the bolt on the door. "The taxis," he said.

There were three of them. Nancy and George got into the first one, with Dr. Stone's luggage piled between them on the seat. The Tarahumara runners rode in the other two. The taxis careened through the narrow streets of Chihuahua, with little regard for traffic signs, pedestrians, or other cars. Soon the driver of Nancy and George's taxi turned onto a broad avenue with a wide boulevard running down the middle, where people strolled beside fountains and under the gaze of bronze statues. Across the street was the train station, an old, ornate building.

The taxi drivers let them all off at the entrance, amid a swirl of people rushing to catch trains. Nancy searched the crowd for Dr. Stone, but she didn't see him.

"Maybe he's on the platform in the station," George suggested. "Or even waiting on the train."

"The platform would be the best place to find

him," Nancy said. "Some of us can wait while the others can check to see if he's already boarded."

"Dr. Stone doesn't strike me as the disappearing type," George said.

"Me neither."

Tasio, Chacho, and Celedonio each took one of Dr. Stone's bags, and they walked into the station. Here the crowd was even thicker. Nancy checked out the huge overhead information board and saw their train listed at Platform 20.

They emerged on the platform at the center of the train. It was long and sleek, with stainless steel cars. Far down toward the end were two cars with glass domes on them for viewing the spectacular scenery of the Copper Canyon.

A conductor examined their tickets and directed them all to the same car. At Nancy's urging, George, Tasio, and the Tarahumaras went to their seats, while she waited on the platform. A few moments later George emerged from the train.

"He's not on the train," she said. "At least, not in his seat or in the car we're in."

Nancy looked up and down the platform. The crowd was thinning as people boarded the train and the friends and family seeing them off filtered back into the station. A half-dozen porters and conductors strolled along the side of the train. Nancy heard the shrill whistle of the train, and jets of steam suddenly gushed from beneath the cars, flooding the platform with mist. One of the conductors raised a whistle to his lips and blew hard.

"Señoritas," another called to them. "We are leaving!" He motioned impatiently toward the open door to the railway car.

"What do we do now?" George muttered.

Nancy turned to the conductor, who once again waved toward the car door. "We're waiting for our traveling companion," Nancy protested.

"But, señorita, the train cannot wait any longer," he said. As if to punctuate his warning, the train's deafening whistle shrilled through the station for the second time. Tasio and Chacho appeared at the open door, searching for Nancy and George.

"There he is!" George shouted.

Nancy turned and saw Bingham Stone staggering up the steps onto the platform, grasping his canvas shoulder bag tightly with one hand. He looked gray and haggard, as if he hadn't slept all night. When he spotted Nancy and George, Nancy could see the relief in his eyes.

Huffing and puffing, he loped up the platform. "Thank goodness," he cried. "I was afraid I'd missed—"

The conductor blew his whistle again. "Señor, señoritas!" he cried. "We cannot wait any longer."

"Come on," Nancy urged Dr. Stone. "Let's get aboard."

They'd barely stepped into the vestibule at the end of the car when the conductor shut the metal door with a loud clang and the train lurched forward. The double seats lining both sides of the aisle were full. Just inside the door, the first four seats on each side had been turned to face each other. Patricio, Vitorio, Celedonio, and Chacho sat opposite one another on one side. Tasio sat on the other side of the aisle, with three empty seats for Nancy, George, and Dr. Stone.

"Ah, I see my luggage made it," Dr. Stone said, eyeing his canvas valises in the overhead rack.

"Dr. Stone, where were you?" Nancy asked, taking her seat. Looking up at him, she saw that his clothes were soiled and spotted with dirt. His eyes were bloodshot and puffy. When he took off his jacket, Nancy noticed a nasty scratch down his right arm, from the elbow to his wrist.

Dr. Stone was looking through his bags, zipping and unzipping them, as if he were inspecting to make sure everything was there.

"Er, ah, something came up," he said, continuing to riffle through his bags. "A professional matter. I'll explain later." Then he stuffed his canvas shoulder bag under the seat and sat down beside Tasio. He gave a huge yawn. "I'm exhausted. I haven't slept a wink all night. I'm sorry to have left you all in the lurch like that. Let me grab a few winks, and I'll explain everything."

Dr. Stone closed his eyes and almost immediately fell asleep. Nancy and George, who were sitting opposite Tasio and Dr. Stone, watched the city of Chihuahua give way to endless sprawling slums and vast landfills that seemed to be populated only with children. Then the desert began, cactus and scrub trees, with small Mexican towns and adobe houses strewn sporadically along the tracks.

They were going uphill, and when the train turned on a long curve, Nancy could make out the mountains ahead of them. They seemed a long way off, but in time the view outside the window turned to that of a stone cliff. The track wound along the side of the mountain, where it had been dynamited. On the far side of the tracks was a deep gorge.

By midmorning it seemed they had stopped climbing, and the train sped across a bridge over a narrow valley, where willows and eucalyptus grew along the banks of a stream. The terrain leveled off, and Nancy saw women in bright shawls and short, colorful skirts walking along a mud road near the edge of a narrow river.

Dr. Stone slept soundly, occasionally interrupting the quiet of the railway car with a spurt of light snoring. The Tarahumara runners were by turns excited or quiet, sometimes pointing at things out the window and speaking animatedly in their own language, other times sitting back to enjoy the beauty of the countryside. Nancy noticed how their faces glowed though, and she guessed it was from happiness at returning home.

Suddenly the train's whistle shrieked, a sound so loud it reverberated through the car. Once, twice, then a third time. Then the train began to brake. The metal wheels screeched horrendously against the tracks, and clouds of hissing steam poured out from beneath the car.

"What's going on?" Nancy asked Tasio, who, with George, was peering out the window. The train was slowing rapidly.

"I'm not sure," Tasio answered.

Nancy leaned over and looked out the window beside George—and caught her breath. A dozen men in blue military uniforms, carrying rifles, stood along the tracks, with several trucks and cars lined up on a gravel road behind them.

"Soldiers!" George exclaimed. "They're stopping the train!"

Chapter

Eleven

I WONDER what's going on," Nancy said. "Those men look like they mean business."

The train slowly screeched to a halt. A worried hubbub arose from all the passengers, who craned their necks to peer out the windows. A young porter walked briskly through the car, telling people in Spanish and English to remain calm.

"Policía federal," he told Nancy and George, when Nancy asked him who the men were. Federal police.

"But why are they stopping the train?" an elderly American woman demanded.

The porter gave an exaggerated shrug and continued on his way through the car. In the seat opposite Nancy and George, Bingham Stone stirred, then suddenly sat upright, blinking to clear his eyes. "Wh-What?" he stammered, as if he'd forgotten where he was. "What's going on?"

"Federal police have stopped the train," Nancy told him. "No one seems to know why."

Instantly, Stone was alert. Nancy noticed that the Tarahumaras were completely silent. Staring out the window, Nancy saw an officer with a visored hat and impressive gold braid on his sleeves walking toward the train. He was tall and had a thin mustache. Nancy noticed that his hand rested on the butt of the gun in the holster at his side. The Tarahumaras crowded over to Nancy's side of the train to peek out the window.

"Colonel Ramirez," Vitorio said, his voice filled with dread. He was gazing at the man with the gold braid on his uniform.

"You know who he is?" Nancy asked.

Tasio nodded grimly. "He is well known in Copper Canyon. He is a man who is better avoided. He does not like Indians."

The head conductor strode through the car, followed by several of his assistants. As he disappeared through the door at the end of the car, several feet away, Nancy heard voices arguing. Tasio rose from his seat and silently moved down the aisle. He stood at the exit door. Nancy peered around the corner to watch him. Clearly, Tasio was listening to the muffled voices outside.

A moment later he returned to his seat. "The

police want to search the train for something, but the conductor insists that they must keep to the schedule. I think the train will be moving again."

"Do you know what they're looking for?" George asked.

Tasio shrugged. "Maybe not something," he said ominously. "Maybe someone."

Just then Nancy saw the police outside suddenly snap to attention. The mustached officer shouted several commands, and the lines of men moved apart. Several boarded the train at different cars, while others returned to the cars parked on the gravel road.

Nancy felt the train hum and then jerk forward. The Tarahumaras returned to their seats across the aisle. Steadily, the train picked up speed. Another conductor, a young one, made his way through the car, apologizing for the inconvenience.

Almost immediately the door opened again. Nancy saw Bingham Stone blanch and shrink into his seat as if hoping he might not be noticed. The police officer with the thin mustache and the gold-trimmed uniform entered. Ramirez, Nancy thought. He was accompanied by several other officers and a red-faced conductor, who seemed annoyed. At least they no longer carried rifles, Nancy noticed, but they wore handguns in holsters at their waists.

Colonel Ramirez and his men stepped into the

aisle and stopped at the seats where Nancy, George, Dr. Stone, and the Tarahumaras were sitting. Nancy saw that the Indians were silent, their faces filled with apprehension. The colonel's eyes flickered across the faces of the four Tarahumaras, then he eyed Nancy, George, and Dr. Stone. Finally, his gaze lingered on Tasio, his face expressionless. Then he gave a signal to his men.

Two officers immediately demanded to see Nancy and George's papers. Nancy took her driver's license from her shoulder bag. "What exactly is the problem?" she asked quietly, handing it over.

The young man ignored her question. Instead, he compared the photograph to Nancy's face. Colonel Ramirez scrutinized her and George.

"Americans." The way the colonel stated it, it was half question, half accusation.

Nancy nodded. "We came to see Copper Canyon."

"A man has been murdered," Colonel Ramirez said in excellent English. "And we are looking for someone suspected of killing him."

"He must have been an important man for you to have to call out a small army of police to stop a train," George commented.

Ramirez eyed her coldly. "He was a very important man," he said firmly.

The young officer handed the driver's license

back to Nancy and took George's. Colonel Ramirez eyed the second officer and jerked his head toward Tasio.

"Your papers!" he ordered in Spanish.

Wordlessly, Tasio handed the man a sheet of folded paper. "My identification papers were stolen yesterday in Chihuahua. I filed a police report, and they gave me this temporary paper."

The police officer handed the paper to Ramirez, who glanced at it quickly. A triumphant smile flickered across his face. "Humada. Tasio Humada. You are the person we have been looking for.

"You're under arrest, Humada," he announced. Ramirez gave a curt nod to his two officers, and they pounced on Tasio. Across the aisle, Chacho and Celedonio rose, about to jump to Tasio's rescue. The conductor moved in front of them, blocking their way. The two officers hauled Tasio from his seat into the aisle. He struggled, but it was useless. Ramirez's men grabbed his arms and snapped handcuffs around his wrists.

"What's going on here!" Dr. Stone thundered. He stood up, his face contorted with rage.

Ramirez stared at Stone calmly. "Bernardo Lupe, owner of the Copcan Logging Corporation, was murdered last night, and we have evidence proving that Tasio Humada is the killer."

"But that's impossible!" Dr. Stone sputtered. "Tasio was in his hotel room last night. I saw him. There are no buses late at night, Tasio can't drive a car, and—"

Colonel Ramirez interrupted Dr. Stone with a confident laugh. "The Tarahumaras can run, can't they? Twenty miles from Chihuahua to Lupe's house. A Tara could run that far in two hours, perhaps less. Isn't that right, Tasio Humada?"

Tasio remained silent.

"But Tasio is a Tarahumara!" Dr. Stone insisted. "He wouldn't murder—"

"That will be for the court to decide," Ramirez said, cutting Stone off again.

"Colonel Ramirez, you mentioned that you had evidence connecting the murder to Tasio," Nancy said politely. "What kind of evidence?"

Ramirez eyed her carefully. "The most incriminating thing possible, señorita. His identification papers. They were on the ground outside Bernardo Lupe's house. Right where he dropped them."

"But his papers were stolen in Chihuahua," Nancy said. "Whoever stole them must have left them there. That's probably your murderer."

Colonel Ramirez's face hardened and he stared at her, his thin lips twitching beneath his mustache. He took a butane lighter from his pocket and held it to the edge of Tasio's temporary papers. Instantly, the paper caught fire. Ramirez held a corner between finger and thumb while the flame reduced it to charred black ash. Before it burned his hand, Ramirez dropped the burning paper. Immediately, he stomped on it, crushing the fire out. Nothing was left of it. Nancy stared at him in horror. Ramirez snickered.

"There is no police report. And no temporary papers," Ramirez said. "All of you are under arrest as accessories. You will be charged with helping this murderer escape!"

"This is preposterous!" Bingham Stone roared.

One of the officers drew his gun and held it on the four Tarahumaras sitting across from each other. A second man grabbed Dr. Stone and twisted his arms behind his back to handcuff him.

"There is a small settlement a dozen miles away," Ramirez told them. "The train will stop there, and we will take you off. You will be kept in jail—"

Suddenly the train braked violently, sending everyone who was standing flying. People in seats jolted back and forth, and the train seemed to teeter precariously on the track. The air was filled with a bone-shattering screech of metal wheels on metal rails.

Then Nancy heard heavy thuds on the roof and

what sounded like feet running up and down the length of it.

"Train robbers!" a passenger shouted hysterically.

Nancy saw Ramirez eye the ceiling of the railroad car and reach for his gun.

Chapter

Twelve

From the corner of her eye Nancy saw two Tarahumaras she hadn't met before, in breechcloths and bare feet, fly into the car. Somewhere, a woman screamed. The first man kicked out, knocking Ramirez's gun aside. The colonel fell back against the seat. The other man wrestled the second officer's gun away from him.

Bingham Stone shoved Nancy aside and attacked the third officer, who turned and swung the butt of his gun down on Dr. Stone's forehead. Stone's eyes rolled up in his head, and he crumpled onto his seat, blood streaming from the wound in his forehead.

More people crowded into the car. The last officer surrendered, dropping his gun. Other passengers confronted the conductors, pushing them farther down the car. A fearful silence was broken only by the sounds of several passengers weeping.

"Quick, George!" Nancy ordered. "I need something to stop the bleeding."

George dug in her backpack and pulled out a clean cotton T-shirt. Nancy pressed it to Stone's forehead, then took his pulse. Although the older man was out cold, his pulse was steady. Still, there was no question that he needed immediate medical attention.

The Tarahumaras were arguing with one another. The newcomers who had stormed the train were shouting at Tasio and the other runners. Tasio's hands were already free, and the handcuffs were now on Ramirez.

Tasio, glowering, made a signal with his hand, and suddenly everyone was silent. He bent over to look at the unconscious anthropologist.

"Is Bing all right?" he asked.

"He needs to see a doctor," Nancy said. "As soon as possible."

"And he will never get one in a Mexican jail," Tasio said grimly, glancing at Ramirez and the other two officers, whose arms were being bound with thick rope.

"I will get him to a doctor, but it will be a difficult journey," Tasio said. "And you will have to come with us."

Nancy studied him warily. "First, you'd better explain what's going on."

Tasio sighed. "This man named Bernardo Lupe, whom Celedonio spoke of earlier and who has been murdered, is a very rich man. And he is the enemy of my people because he cuts down the trees in our forests." For a moment Tasio's voice became emotional. "Now they want people to think I am his murderer. I am being put in a picture, as you Americans say."

"Put in a pic— Oh, you mean framed," George said.

Tasio nodded and gestured toward two of the people who had boarded the train. "Juan and Valencio tell me that someone who is friendly to the Tarahumaras warned my friends that they would try to arrest me for it."

"But your papers," George said. "They were stolen yesterday. We saw it, I mean, we were there. . . ." Her voice trailed off.

Tasio looked at her calmly. "Now I believe someone stole my papers so they could frame me for this murder. Then Ramirez destroyed the temporary papers so he would have additional grounds to arrest me. And," Tasio continued, "I think if we go back to Chihuahua, we would find that there is no longer a police report, either. You must believe me: It is impossible for me to have killed this man. But we are in great danger—you as well as my friends and myself. We must leave this train immediately and travel to safety with my people."

"Why do *we* have to go?" George asked, astonished.

"Because Colonel Ramirez will jail you as accessories to the crime, since you are traveling with me," Tasio said. "And in jail, anything might happen to you."

He turned to Ramirez, handcuffed in the seat where the Tarahumaras had been sitting. Ramirez scowled back. "This man would gladly kill *all* of us if it suits his purposes," Tasio said.

Looking at Tasio, Nancy thought of the night before, when Tasio had returned to the hotel, hot and sweaty from a mysterious run. Where *had* he been at five o'clock in the morning? she wondered. Could he be the murderer?

"If you run away from the law now," Nancy said, stalling, "you'll just make people think you are guilty."

"Perhaps this is not the solution I would have chosen, but my friends have gone to much trouble to rescue me." Tasio flashed a wary smile. "So it is better to enjoy the good luck. We must hurry and leave now."

"And what if we don't want to go?" George asked.

"You have no choice," Tasio said. "Really, you must trust me."

Juan, Valencio, and several other Tarahumaras who had boarded the train began speaking at once to Tasio in their own language, and Nancy saw them gesturing outside. Two of them started to lift Bingham Stone, but Nancy stopped them. "You can't take him anywhere unless he's on a stretcher."

Tasio nodded. "You are right." He turned to the young conductor, who was sitting under the watchful eyes of several men. "Is there a stretcher on the train?"

The conductor pointed nervously to the end of the car, where a white metal case was marked with a large red cross. Tasio gave orders. Juan and Valencio opened the cabinet and found a collapsible stretcher. A few moments later they had assembled the canvas stretcher with its aluminum frame.

Gently, they placed Dr. Stone on the stretcher. Then Celedonio and Patricio carried him outside. Nancy and George rose from their seats and followed, the Tarahumaras closing around them in the vestibule of the railway car.

"What about our luggage?" George asked, moving toward the door with Nancy.

"We cannot carry it," Tasio said simply.

Nancy stepped down onto the gravel siding and looked around. They were perched on a promontory over a great chasm, surrounded by mountains on all sides. Except for the railroad track and the train, there was no sign of civilization.

"My question is," George said as she joined Nancy, "are we prisoners? Or are we hostages?"

"Neither," Nancy said grimly. "We're fugitives from the law!"

Chapter

Thirteen

DO YOU GET THE FEELING we're wearing out our welcome?" Joe asked Frank after lunch on Tuesday. "Dick doesn't seem to want us here, and I'm getting tired of good ol' Uncle Marcus's fake friendliness."

"I know what you mean," Frank said as the two brothers sat in the living room of the hacienda. "I feel like we're in a kind of limbo. This doesn't seem like a vacation, and we're not getting any cooperation from Dick or Uncle Marcus in trying to find out who might want to hurt Cory. And Cory says he doesn't have an enemy in the world, which is what the few ranch hands we've talked to say. It's frustrating." Idly Frank picked up a TV remote from the side table and turned on the television. There was video footage of a stalled train, blocked by a huge pile of boulders across the tracks.

"In the Copper Canyon region of northern Mexico, there has been a train robbery," the newscaster stated. "Tarahumara Indians pushed boulders onto the track, and when the train came to a stop, they boarded and robbed passengers, overpowering several police officers who were searching for an escaped killer. Details are sketchy, but several Americans are reported missing. In other news . . ."

"What!" Frank exclaimed, sitting up straight.

"Could that be the train Nancy and George are on?" Joe wondered aloud. "They said they were leaving Chihuahua for Copper Canyon this morning, right?"

"Right," Frank said. "So unless there's more than one train a day . . ." He reached for the telephone just as Rita entered the hacienda.

"I came to see if you wanted to go horse-back—" Rita stopped speaking when she saw the expression on Joe's face. "Joe, what is it? Is something wrong?"

Joe quickly explained, while Frank punched Amtrak's 800 number, which he knew by heart. All he got was a busy signal. He pressed the redial button. When the number was still busy, he banged down the receiver in frustration. "We've got to find out if they're all right!" he exclaimed.

"Mr. Weston and Dick flew down to Copper Canyon this morning," Rita said. "To Creel, a small town right in the middle of Tarahumara country. They have business there."

Just then Cory walked in the front door. "Why do you guys want to know where my father and brother went?" he asked sharply. "I wish you'd stop investigating or whatever you're doing. I keep telling you, that falling boulder was an accident. And you're making my dad even more paranoid than he already is."

"Cory, this isn't about what happened during the marathon," Frank said quickly, and then brought Cory up to date. "Since Creel is right in the middle of the Copper Canyon area," he concluded, "do you think we could call your dad to see if he can find Nancy and George?"

Cory was apologetic. "Sorry for snapping at you," he said. "Dad always carries a cellular phone with him. I know he'll do whatever he can to help."

Cory picked up the phone and punched in a number. Frank motioned his brother to the far side of the room, out of hearing distance. "I don't like the feel of this," he told Joe in a low voice. "Finding the same kind of writing paper that the threatening letters to Tasio were written on might be a coincidence. The fact that the Westons are having trouble getting lumber and Tasio has protested against logging interests could also be a coincidence, I guess. But now Marcus and Dick

Weston are down in Tarahumara country, and I'm sure there's a connection."

Joe nodded. "I think we should go to Copper Canyon and get to the bottom of this before Tasio gets hurt."

"Or Nancy and George," Frank added ominously.

Cory hung up the telephone. "Dad says there's only one train a day that leaves Chihuahua for Copper Canyon," he told Frank and Joe. "If Nancy and George were on it this morning, then they were on the train that got robbed. But he's going to have one of his people check the passenger list—"

"I'll cancel the plans for our ride," Rita said, heading for the door. "I'll tell the wranglers to unsaddle the horses."

She returned a few minutes later just as the phone rang. Cory picked it up and listened carefully. Then he said, "Thanks, Dad," and hung up. He turned to Frank and Joe. "Nancy and George are on the passenger list, along with Dr. Stone, and they're listed as missing."

"Missing!" Joe hissed. "How can they be missing?"

Cory shrugged. "Dad didn't have any more details, but he said that when they turn up, he'll be one of the first to know."

"We have to go there," Frank said simply.

Joe nodded. "How far is it?"

"It is a long way," Rita said, moving closer to Joe. She looked at Cory. "Perhaps . . ." Her voice trailed off.

Cory cleared his throat. "I can fly you guys down. I mean, we could all go. There's another airplane down on the landing strip, and a pilot to go with it." He looked from Frank to Joe. "All I have to do is call down there."

Frank's eyes lit up. "Great idea."

"When can we leave?" Joe demanded.

"As soon as you're packed," Cory said. He reached for the phone and made arrangements. As he hung up, he said, "We'll be in Creel before sunset."

An hour later the Hardys were on the landing strip, where a small twin-prop airplane was ready for takeoff. The pilot was a taciturn man wearing aviator sunglasses. He sat at the controls, chewing on a toothpick. Joe unloaded their bags from the Land Rover, while Frank carried them onto the plane and Cory hobbled behind on his crutches. Rita watched from Cory's pickup. When they were finished, Joe walked over to say goodbye.

"Good luck finding your friends," Rita said through the open window. When Joe put his hand on the windowsill, Rita rested hers on top and squeezed it gently.

"Thanks," Joe answered. "It's probably just some mix-up that they're listed as missing."

"I hope so." Rita paused and looked shyly away, then back at Joe. "Is Nancy your girlfriend? Or George?"

"Nancy?" Joe said, surprised. "No, Nancy and George are old friends of mine."

Rita smiled, her warm, dark eyes holding Joe's in a long, affectionate gaze. "I hope you are coming back to the Double W for a few days before you go home."

A big smile spread across Joe's face, and he brushed his hand through his short blond hair. "Are you kidding? Of course we'll be back! You owe me a horseback ride." With that, Joe leaned into the window of the pickup and kissed Rita.

Rita gently touched his cheek. "Go and catch your plane now," she said softly, smiling again. "I hope you'll return soon."

Joe squeezed her hand, turned, and ran across the gravel runway toward the small aircraft just as the propellers began turning. He climbed aboard and sat in the rear seat beside Cory. Frank sat with the pilot.

They taxied down the airstrip. Joe watched the ground below drop away, then followed the truck with Rita at the wheel as it climbed the mountainside back to the Weston residence. The desert mountains, streaked with the long, straight roads, looked like the surface of a shriveled prune.

When they passed over the Mexican border,

Cory pointed out a long fence below. "That marks the border," he said. The landscape grew progressively rougher, the mountains higher, the ravines between the ranges deeper and darker.

When the pilot finally announced they were arriving at Creel, the sun was setting and the horizon had taken on a canary yellow glow. Frank and Joe could make out vast cleared areas below where the forest had been razed. Then the airplane passed over sawmills, with mountains of logs piled around tin-roofed buildings.

Cory led them through customs in the tiny Creel airport—scarcely a shed with a customs inspector's desk—while the pilot taxied the airplane to a nearby hangar, a steel Quonset hut. Marcus and Dick Weston were waiting for them there. Cory's father greeted his son with a warm embrace but gazed grimly at the Hardys.

"Beautiful country down here," Mr. Weston said. "Too bad you're here under these circumstances."

"What's the word, sir?" Joe asked.

Mr. Weston shook his head. "The train is blocked about eight miles up a rugged ravine. They had to run the passengers into Creel in army trucks, and they still haven't got all the people off."

"Them renegade Indians took some American hostages," Dick added. "Might've been your friends Nancy and George."

"Now, we don't know that," Marcus Weston admonished his elder son.

"Can we go out to where the train is?" Frank asked. "Maybe we can help—"

Marcus Weston put his hands up to quiet Frank. "I've made an appointment with the chief of police. He's waiting for us at headquarters right now. So why don't you ask him, and maybe he'll arrange for it."

He led Frank and Joe to two Land Rovers waiting outside the tiny air station. Cory, hobbling on his crutches, followed with Dick.

As they approached the Land Rovers, Frank recognized Sam and Ernie, the two bodyguards, one at the wheel of each vehicle. They drove into Creel, arriving in the small mountain town just as lights were coming on in buildings.

Creel had the look of a pioneer western town, Frank thought, with log buildings fronting the main street. They came to a stop outside an ornate stucco building, where a backlit sign announced *Policía*. Several uniformed men opened a huge iron gate, and the cars drove through into a spacious cobblestone courtyard.

Marcus Weston led Frank, Joe, and his two sons into the building and up a broad flight of stairs that Cory managed with difficulty. On the second floor they waited on hard benches, under high, beamed ceilings, as police officers strode noisily around them. Finally a paneled door opened, and a man wearing an expensive suit appeared. His eyes lit up when he saw Marcus Weston.

"My apologies, Mr. Weston, for keeping you waiting," he said, clasping Marcus Weston's hand.

Weston slapped the man lightly on the back. "No problem, Esteban," Marcus Weston said, back to his usual jovial self. "You know my son Dick, and this is my son Cory." Then he pointed to the Hardys. "These here young fellas are Frank and Joe Hardy, and they believe their friends were on that train that got hijacked today. They came down here to see if they could help out."

"Esteban Maracas, chief of police," the man said, standing aside and holding the door wider. "Please come in."

As Frank and Joe entered, they noticed a second man in the room. He was tall, with a thin mustache, and wore a starched uniform with gold braid on the sleeves and at the collar.

"This is Colonel Ramirez," the police chief said, making a casual introduction. "He was on the train when the Tarahumaras boarded it and began taking prisoners." Maracas paused. "And for a time Colonel Ramirez became their prisoner."

Frank could see the uniformed police officer

visibly stiffen. "We were overwhelmed," he said in a low, dignified tone, but Frank could sense the man's anger.

"Please sit," the police chief instructed, gesturing to a long couch and several chairs that faced his desk. "Colonel Ramirez estimates that more than fifty Tarahumaras were involved." Maracas sat behind his desk and paused for a moment. "It seems like a rather large number," he continued, glancing in Ramirez's direction. "However, there were sufficient Indians to disarm him and two other officers."

Frank cleared his throat, then spoke. "What word do you have of Nancy Drew or George Fayne? Why can't anyone tell us where they are?"

"Your friends were indeed on the train," Colonel Ramirez said almost smugly, still glaring at the chief of police. "But we don't know where they are now."

"More correctly," the chief of police interjected, "we know they are somewhere in the mountains of Copper Canyon."

Frank stood up and strode to the front of the police chief's desk. He put his hands on the polished surface and leaned toward the man. "We'd like some straight answers," he said firmly. "Where are Nancy and George?"

"Kidnapped," the chief of police replied. "They were taken prisoner by the Tarahumara Indians and marched into the wilderness."

Chapter

Fourteen

PRISONERS! BUT WHY?" Frank demanded.

The chief of police shrugged lightly. "A young man named Tasio Humada has just been arrested for the murder of—"

"Tasio!" Joe interrupted in surprise.

"You know this man?" the police chief asked, at once suspicious of Joe.

"From the Cactus Marathon," Joe answered. "We both ran in it."

The police chief nodded. "The Tarahumaras are famed for their running. This time, however, Señor Humada's ability to run has got him into trouble."

"Who was murdered?" Frank asked.

"A prominent citizen named Bernardo Lupe,"

Colonel Ramirez replied. "Humada ran from Chihuahua to Lupe's home outside the city and murdered him. But he stupidly dropped his identification papers in Lupe's yard."

"Why would Tasio want to murder this man?" Joe asked. "I mean, what was his motive?"

"Lupe owned logging rights on land that the Tarahumaras claim," Marcus Weston said. "The Tarahumaras tied him up in court for a year, and this young fella, Tasio, led the campaign for his people. But Lupe won. He got the permits he needed and was about to start logging."

"Yeah, and we're supposed to be buying those logs when they cut the trees down," Dick Weston added. "'Cept now that Lupe's dead, it's all tied up legally. Humada knew that would happen, so that's got to be why he killed the guy."

"And we knew he was on the train back to Copper Canyon when we tried to arrest him," Colonel Ramirez added. "We intended to take him by surprise. Somehow word must have leaked out. They escaped and took your friends as hostages."

"What are you doing to find them?" Joe demanded.

"Everything we can," Ramirez assured him. "We have helicopters flying in grids over the area. They're in constant radio contact, so when they find them, I'll know immediately."

"That still doesn't explain why they took Nancy and George as hostages," Frank pointed out.

"Bargaining chips, Frank!" Marcus Weston bellowed. "Bargaining chips. As long as they have a couple of gringo tourists with them, it'll stop the police from closing in."

Frank shook his head slowly, still in disbelief. "If that's true," he said, "Tasio's in trouble. Nancy and George will be more trouble than they're worth."

Marcus Weston had arranged rooms for Frank and Joe at the Creel Inn, an old, rambling building made of rustic logs and filled with brightly painted Mexican furniture. After dinner with the Westons, Frank and Joe decided to make it an early night and returned to their room.

When Joe came out of the shower, he noticed Frank glancing through a guidebook. "How's your Spanish, Frank?"

"So-so," Frank said. "We can probably get by."

"What do you say we head off by ourselves tomorrow morning and wander around Creel?" Joe suggested. "See what we can dig up."

"What about Cory? And the other Westons?"

Joe's muffled voice came from under the towel as he dried his hair. "I think we can operate more efficiently on our own," he said. Then he pulled the towel aside and looked at his brother. "The Westons might cramp our style."

Frank smiled. "I know what you mean. As I said before, Uncle Marcus's 'friendliness' is really beginning to get to me."

"Right," Joe agreed. "And there's no free lunch. He wants something from us."

Frank gave Joe a questioning look. "What do you mean?"

This time all Joe could do was shrug. "I don't know exactly. I keep getting the feeling that he's overdoing the hospitality bit to sidetrack us somehow. I just wish I knew from what."

"I know what you mean," Frank said. "I keep thinking about those threatening letters Tasio received that match the stationery at the hacienda. I've been wondering if maybe Dick Weston sent those letters."

"Interesting idea," Joe mused. "What makes you think so? And why?"

"Because the letters *sound* like Dick," Frank said. "The way Dick always sounds aggressive when he talks, but kind of juvenile, too. Like he's still twelve and not twenty-two."

Joe stopped drying himself and thought for a moment. "You know, that makes a lot of sense. Remember the bad grammar and spelling in those letters? Dick's grammar isn't too hot, either."

"As for why," Frank said, "you heard the

Westons say they did business deals with this Bernardo Lupe. Tasio Humada would be in the way, too." He gave a deep sigh. "I'll tell you one thing," Frank went on, "Tasio Humada didn't strike me as the murdering type."

Joe smiled. "Probably most murderers don't seem like killers before they commit a crime. And especially someone who murders for what he believes is a just cause."

"You're right," Frank said. Then he somberly added, "If he *is* the murderer, then he *could* be holding Nancy and George as hostages."

"And that means they could be in serious trouble," Joe said.

Frank nodded. "This whole situation makes me uneasy. The sooner we start investigating, the better I'll feel. In the afternoon we can take advantage of the Westons' offer to fly us over Copper Canyon."

"Sounds good to me," Joe said. "We need to find out more about Bernardo Lupe and his murder." He pulled back the covers and got into bed. "It's like putting a puzzle together. Except that we don't have all the pieces."

On Wednesday morning the Hardys had barely gotten up when the Westons knocked on their door and invited them to breakfast. Dick Weston, as usual, was moody, but Cory chatted on about Creel and Copper Canyon.

137

Over enormous plates of thick bacon, fried eggs, fresh tortillas, and hot, spicy, refried beans, Marcus Weston told them he'd arranged for a helicopter at one o'clock that afternoon.

"We're not going to stop looking for them," he assured the Hardys. "Alive or—" He caught himself and quickly swallowed an enormous forkful of home fries.

"Er, Uncle Marcus," Joe said, "you know Nancy was traveling with a friend of her dad, Dr. Bingham Stone, and he sponsored the Tarahumara runners in Tucson."

"Stone," Weston grunted between mouthfuls, nodding as he chewed.

"The guy's a traitor," Dick muttered, attacking the flapjacks on his plate. "A traitor to his country," he said, a note of satisfaction in his voice.

"How so?" Frank asked sharply. "That's a pretty serious accusation."

"Oh, he doesn't mean anything by it," Marcus Weston interjected, wiping his lips with a thick cloth napkin. "Dr. Stone goes around encouraging the Tarahumaras to make land claims and such. He's the one who started a bunch of Jesuit priests educating the brightest of them. And he was behind their protest against the loggers."

"We were supposed to buy logs from Lupe for the mill," Dick said. "We don't get the logs we need, we'll have to close it down. Throw eighty

Americans out of work. And that's why Bingham Stone is a traitor."

"But you said the Tarahumaras lost their claim," Joe pointed out. "What's stopping you from buying the logging rights now?"

"It's Mexico," Cory Weston said simply.

"I don't understand," Frank said.

Marcus Weston waved his fork in the air. "The claim was to log on national land, and it was in Bernardo Lupe's name. Now it will have to be assigned to someone else. Money passed hands to make sure the Tarahumaras lost in court and that claim stayed in Lupe's name."

"You mean the court case was fixed!" Joe exclaimed.

"You bet it was fixed," Dick Weston said. "But now that Lupe's dead, the Tarahumaras stand a fighting chance to stop the logging altogether."

After breakfast Marcus Weston proposed they drive out to the landing strip and inspect the helicopter waiting to fly them over Copper Canyon. "I won't take no for an answer," he insisted.

Frank and Joe returned to their room to collect their jackets. "Do you get the feeling the Westons don't want us out of their sight?" Joe asked as they walked down the hallway toward their room. "Cory's dad didn't even give us a chance to make plans," he complained. "And what's the point of looking at a helicopter we'll be flying in this afternoon?"

"Yeah," Frank agreed. "Something's not right."

As they entered their room, Frank found an envelope that had been slid under the door. It bore a police insignia. "What's this?" he wondered aloud, turning it over in his hands.

"We'll never find out if you don't open it," Joe said.

Frank was silent as he read the short note inside. "If my Spanish is correct, the police want us to claim Nancy and George's luggage. It's been taken to the police station. I guess Uncle Marcus told the chief of police where we're staying."

Joe snapped his fingers excitedly. "That's our out!" he exclaimed. "Let's leave a note at the desk that we had to pick up the luggage and that we'll meet them at noon in time for the helicopter ride. We don't have to tell them where the bags are. That way, they won't know where to find us."

Frank nodded as he folded the letter and stuffed it into his pocket. "You're on, Joe," he said, and headed for the door.

They descended the stairs to the first floor and left a message with the desk clerk. They were about to exit through the front doors when they heard Marcus Weston's blustering voice coming down the corridor. Frank motioned Joe to follow him into the restaurant. It was empty, except for a lone waiter changing tablecloths. Frank and Joe crossed the restaurant and exited through a side door.

At the police station, a bored duty officer scrutinized the note Frank showed him, then pointed to the stairs. "Detective Garcia," he said.

Frank and Joe ascended the staircase. An empty corridor ran the length of the building. Frank spotted an open office door and leaned inside. A handsome, dark-haired man was seated at a desk, where he was reading a voluminous report. When he noticed the Hardys, he stood up and came around his desk.

Frank held up the letter. "Detective Joaquin Garcia?"

The detective smiled, revealing ivory white teeth. *"Sí,"* he said, waving Frank and Joe inside. His eyes flitted across the letter, and he nodded in understanding.

"You are the friends of the missing American women," he said, returning to his desk and lowering himself into his chair. He pointed to the far corner of the office, where several valises, backpacks, and a large green canvas shoulder bag had been piled. Frank and Joe recognized Nancy and George's luggage immediately.

"I took personal responsibility for it," the

detective said. "Sometimes valuable things disappear mysteriously in these situations."

"We appreciate your concern," Frank replied, inspecting the baggage quickly. He noticed that some had tags with Bingham Stone's name on them.

Joe looked at Detective Garcia. "Why do you think the Tarahumaras kidnapped our friends?"

The man stared at Joe for a long moment without answering, as if sizing him up. Then he leaned back in his chair and crossed his hands behind his head. "One of the men is wanted for murder," he said slowly. "Unfortunately, your friends are their hostages. That is the official explanation."

He looked at Frank and Joe, almost as if expecting them to challenge him. After a moment of silence, Garcia continued. "Of course, it is very unusual for a Tarahumara to commit murder. In fact, it is unheard of."

"Never?" Frank questioned in disbelief.

Garcia shrugged. "In war, of course. And the Tarahumaras drink a kind of powerful beer that intoxicates them. Sometimes, in such a condition, a fight breaks out and a man is killed. But even then, in Tara culture, it is so unusual that they believe the killer was possessed by demons, forces beyond his control. In those circumstances, he is not even punished. So for a Tara to go out of his way to kill someone . . ."

Garcia sat forward in his chair and began shuffling papers on his desk.

"Are you suggesting—" Frank started.

"I'm merely telling you the results of the police investigation into the murder of Bernardo Lupe. Tasio Humada is charged with the crime," Garcia said very officially. Finally he stopped shuffling papers and raised his eyes to the Hardys.

"I was brought up in Creel. My father is Mexican, but my mother is Tarahumara," he told them. "I can say nothing except what I am instructed to say."

Frank nodded. Detective Garcia obviously was in disagreement with his superiors. Frank realized that if he and Joe were going to know what the truth was, they'd clearly have to read between the lines.

"I can tell you one thing," Garcia continued. "I don't know why your friends have gone—or been taken—into Copper Canyon. But I do not believe they are in danger. When we find them, I think they will be safe." Garcia sighed. "I fear, however, for Tasio Humada and his friends."

"Why?" Joe asked sharply.

"Several hundred soldiers of the Guardia Nacional are searching Copper Canyon under the command of Colonel Ramirez. Humada is wanted for murder, and his friends have helped him to escape. Ramirez will care little if he finds them alive—or dead."

"But what if Tasio didn't kill Lupe?" Joe asked. "He's got to have a chance to prove his innocence."

"Humada's identification papers were found in the mud below a window, outside the house where the murder took place," Detective Garcia told them. "And footprints as if he had squatted there, waiting for his chance."

"But that's only circumstantial," Frank said. "Someone else could have dropped the papers there."

Detective Garcia smiled politely. "Mexico has a different system of justice than that in your country."

"So I've heard," Joe muttered.

"Here, when a person is charged with a criminal offense, he is considered guilty until he proves he is innocent," Garcia continued. "And sometimes, even then . . ." He shrugged.

"It's the question of motive that bothers me," Frank said.

"Bernardo Lupe claimed the right to log forests on Tarahumara land," Garcia stated simply. "Tasio Humada had sworn publicly to stop him."

Frank paced to the window and peered out over the street, where a few pedestrians strolled along the narrow sidewalk. He turned around and faced Garcia. "Can you get us into Tarahumara country?" he asked suddenly. "We need a guide."

Joe looked at his brother, puzzled. "What for? We can fly over in Weston's chopper."

"If your friends are with Tasio Humada and the Tarahumaras," Garcia said, "you will never see them from the air. In those canyons they can hear a helicopter coming when it is miles away. Plenty of time to cover their trail and hide."

"Exactly." Frank nodded. "Tasio and the other Tarahumaras didn't flee into the mountains just to get lost. They went there because it's their home. It's where their friends are."

Joe saw what Frank was getting at. "Right," he said. "And other Tarahumaras might know where they are."

Detective Garcia looked at them steadily, his face expressionless. Then, abruptly, he stood up, as if he had reached a decision. "I think you are right," he said. "I think that will be the best way to find your friends."

"You can do it?" Joe said eagerly.

"Perhaps," Garcia said vaguely.

Almost as an afterthought, Frank asked, "Do you have a picture of Bernardo Lupe?"

The detective nodded. "Of course." He reached for one of the files stacked in a metal tray on his desk and took a photograph from it. He handed it to Frank.

Frank saw it had been taken at the scene of the crime. The dead man's body was sprawled on the ground, the chest covered with blood. The face was clearly recognizable. Lupe's mouth was open, and one of his front teeth was made of silver.

Joe peeked over Frank's shoulder. "It's the same guy who flew into the Double W the day before yesterday," he said. "The one Marcus Weston was arguing with!"

Chapter

Fifteen

For most of Tuesday, Tasio, the other Tara-humaras, Nancy, and George traveled deeper and deeper into the rugged mountains of Copper Canyon, away from civilization. The men took turns carrying Dr. Stone, who was still unconscious, on the stretcher. At one point Celedonio raced off, returning an hour later smiling happily and carrying a homemade torch of hemp and tar.

"Celedonio went to a cave to find the torch," Tasio explained to Nancy. "It will be safe to stay the night there. And we will have food."

It took them another three hours of rugged travel, scrambling up along the rocky edges of the canyon, to reach their destination. Cliffs, craggy and split by eons of time, rose above them like the crumbling stone walls of ancient fortresses.

Tasio led them into a narrow cave that went back more than thirty feet, then opened into a round, low-ceilinged chamber. Celedonio's torch flickered, whipping shadows back and forth along the rough stone walls. Great black splotches of soot covered the ceiling, the result of dozens of fires that had been built in the chamber.

Patricio and Vitorio came into the cave carrying the stretcher, with Bingham Stone still unconscious. They set him down near the wall of the cave, not far from a ledge where blackened red clay jars had been stacked, along with waist-high wicker baskets.

Nancy knelt beside Dr. Stone and felt his pulse. It was steady, as was his breathing. The man had a terrible cut and swollen bump on his head, however, and Nancy was worried. He needed medical attention. Now that they had stopped for the night, she thought, she would make Tasio answer some questions.

The Tarahumaras found food—venison jerky and pine nuts—stored in the clay jars. Vitorio and Patricio disappeared momentarily and returned carrying a basketful of orange-red fruit that Vitorio said came from a cactus. He carefully cut the spines from the shiny skins and laid them out with the rest of the food. Nancy and George were so hungry it looked like a feast.

Tasio built a small fire near the entrance of the cave so most of the smoke could escape. He boiled water in a clay pot and added a handful of leaves and bark that Patricio had brought back. He held the steaming liquid under Dr. Stone's nose so the doctor breathed in the vapor.

Almost immediately, Dr. Stone stirred, and his eyelids fluttered open. As he looked at Nancy, he whispered her name.

"Drink this," Tasio said, bringing the edge of the clay pot to Dr. Stone's lips. "It will give you strength."

After a few sips Dr. Stone sighed and leaned back, as if exhausted from the mild effort of drinking. Tasio left Nancy alone with him and went to rejoin his friends by the fire.

"Wh-Where are we?" Stone asked finally.

"In the mountains of Copper Canyon," Nancy said. "Tasio brought us to a cave."

Stone seemed satisfied. He nodded his head slightly and closed his eyes again. "Tasio knows what to do."

"Dr. Stone, why were you late for the train this morning?" Nancy asked. "Where did you go?"

Dr. Stone's eyelids fluttered again but stayed closed. "Camera," he replied weakly. "Get—the camera."

Nancy was surprised by his strange answer. "George's camera?" she asked, remembering that it had disappeared from their hotel room in Chihuahua.

Almost imperceptibly, Dr. Stone nodded. "Weston," he said. He took a shallow breath. "Wes—ton." Then he lapsed once again into unconsciousness.

George approached and asked, "Is he all right?"

Nancy shook her head as she tucked the blanket around the anthropologist. "He's very weak." She told her friend what Dr. Stone had said.

"But how can we get my camera?" George asked. "If the guy who was following us in Chihuahua is the one who stole it, there's no way we'll ever get it back."

"I agree," Nancy said with a sigh. "And I don't know why he'd want us to get your camera or why he said 'Weston.'"

"I wonder if he meant Cory," George thought aloud. "Or maybe his dad. Dr. Stone didn't seem too happy when Cory told him at the race who his father was."

Nancy ran her fingers through her hair distractedly. "I could just scream, I'm getting so upset! Dr. Stone wakes up, says some things that don't make any sense, and then he's out of it again." She paused a moment, thinking. "What

I'd like to know is where Dr. Stone was the night Bernardo Lupe was murdered. Where was he just before he turned up at the train station?"

"Why? Do you think he went to Lupe's house, killed him, and returned in time to catch the train?" George asked.

Nancy thought a moment. "I can't rule out any possibilities."

"There's also that priest who came to the hotel in Chihuahua," George reminded her. "The one who was having an argument with Dr. Stone."

"And there's Tasio," Nancy said quietly. She told George about seeing him silently creep into the Chihuahua hotel at daybreak.

George glanced behind her, making sure the Tarahumaras were out of hearing distance. "Do you really think he killed that guy? I mean, what about his lost papers?"

"I know," Nancy said. "But he had motive. And he had opportunity. And it's possible the police found his papers and returned them that night, before he left the hotel." She was silent for a moment, thinking. "As much as I hate to admit it," Nancy said at last, "until Tasio or Dr. Stone volunteers an alibi, either of them might be a murderer. And if that's the case, we could be in danger."

"We'll keep our eyes and ears open, and watch out for each other," George said.

Nancy agreed. "I'm going to try to get some answers from Tasio."

"Just be careful," George warned. "If he *is* the killer, we'll never get out of here alive." She shivered at the thought. "We need him to get us back to civilization."

"I know," Nancy said. "I'll be careful."

Tasio and Chacho had briefly left the cave. Now they reentered, carrying armfuls of dried grass, which they arranged into beds for Nancy and George. On top of the dried grass they put handwoven woolen blankets that they found in some of the large baskets.

Nancy had no chance to question Tasio. He and the other Tarahumaras immediately went to sleep on the cave's cold, bare floor.

When Nancy awoke the next morning, she immediately realized how deeply she'd slept, despite the cold air and hard ground. But the questions she had for Tasio were still very much on her mind.

She walked to the cave entrance, the wool blanket pulled tightly around her, and peered out over the wide canyon bottom. The low eastern sunlight highlighted the variations of color and texture in the stone cliffs opposite her. This was one of the most beautiful places she'd ever seen —and one of the most remote. Civilization could be hundreds of miles away for all she knew.

That thought both excited and terrified her. She was in paradise, but was she sharing it with a murderer? Neither Tasio nor Dr. Stone seemed to have a concrete alibi for where he had been the night Bernardo Lupe was murdered, and they both had a strong motive, for they were both involved in the same cause. True, Dr. Stone was her father's friend, but that didn't mean she could rule him out as a suspect.

Suddenly a new possibility occurred to her. Had Dr. Stone and Tasio plotted *together* to kill Lupe?

Nancy sensed movement behind her, and turned to see Tasio silently emerge from the cave. Startled, she couldn't hide the shudder that ran through her.

He looked at her strangely. "You jumped like a small animal that feels danger," he said.

She mustered a small laugh. "It's nothing," she replied. "I didn't think anyone else was up." To change the subject, Nancy asked, "How did you know this cave was here?"

"My people have lived in caves since the First Man and First Woman. Since the beginning of time," he answered. "There are many in Copper Canyon. Some belong to a particular family, and others, such as this one, are for everyone to use."

Nancy took a deep breath. She had to get Tasio to talk about the murder, and this was her chance. "Tasio, I need to know what's going on," she said quietly. For a moment she thought she saw an uncharacteristic trace of bitterness flash in his eyes.

Without looking at her, Tasio said, "Colonel Ramirez is the sworn enemy of the Tarahumara. And the murdered man, Bernardo Lupe, illegally cut trees on thousands of acres of our land. Whenever my people complained to the police, Ramirez protected Lupe. And he has grown rich doing so."

"Tasio," Nancy said. "Look at me."

The Tarahumara Indian regarded her, his dark eyes glittering and impenetrable.

"Tuesday morning when you came back to the hotel," Nancy said, "you saw me. I know you did. And you know I saw you."

Tasio remained silent, his face blank.

"Where had you been?" Nancy persisted. She realized she might be on dangerous ground, but she needed answers. "You looked like you had run a long way."

She watched as his eyes turned even darker. "Perhaps all the way to the home of Bernardo Lupe?" he asked, his voice tinged with sarcasm.

"I didn't say that," Nancy replied quickly. She didn't want to agitate Tasio. "I just asked where you had been," she said calmly.

"I ran deep into the mountains outside Chihuahua and back," he said. "After dinner I slept. I was sad that my money and papers had been stolen. When I woke up in the middle of the night, I still thought of what a bad day it had been. So I decided to run. I ran for almost three hours."

He looked at Nancy, his eyes searching her face for some reaction. "Of course no one saw me," he said in a low voice. "And I think that whoever stole my money really wanted my papers so they could be left beside this murdered man."

"You mean someone wants to send you to jail so you won't cause any more trouble for them?" Nancy speculated.

"I cannot prove this, of course," Tasio said. "And I do not think they want to send me to jail, either."

"Then what?" Nancy asked.

Tasio was silent a moment. "Sometimes when people are arrested by Colonel Ramirez, they try to escape and are shot and killed."

For a moment Nancy didn't realize what he was getting at—then it hit her. "Someone wants to use Colonel Ramirez to kill you?"

Tasio shrugged. "One man has already been killed," he pointed out. "I don't know why. What was important to my friends was that I not become one of Ramirez's victims. That I was not left alone in his hands."

Nancy listened, without making a judgment. Now there were two versions of the same story. In the police version, Tasio was a dangerous perpetrator. In Tasio's version, he was a victim and in great danger from the police.

"What about Father Sebastien?" Nancy asked. "I heard him and Dr. Stone arguing."

Tasio scowled. "You must forget you heard that or that you even saw us talking together," he told her sharply.

Nancy was surprised at the sudden transformation. She had obviously hit a nerve.

"If you know what is best for you," Tasio continued, "for everyone, just forget it." He turned to reenter the cave.

"We have to get Dr. Stone to a hospital," Nancy said. "I hope that's what we're doing today."

Tasio spoke without turning around. "Today, no. But I think it is important to take you, George, and Dr. Stone to a *ranchería* as soon as possible so you can leave Copper Canyon. I will stay in these mountains as long as I have to."

"Alone?" Nancy asked.

Tasio faced her again. "Copper Canyon is filled with Tarahumaras."

Nancy heard a noise, then watched George emerge from the cave yawning, her blanket draped over her shoulders. A thin line of smoke trickled out from the entrance, and Nancy smelled a wood fire.

Then Nancy heard a noise on the path below the cave. When she turned, she saw a smiling

Vitorio emerge from the oak trees carrying a line of small silver fish.

"We shall eat a good breakfast," he said.

They ate a simple meal of pine nuts and fish, which Vitorio steamed in a clay pot with a perforated bottom that fit into another clay pot filled with boiling water. Dr. Stone was barely conscious, and apparently delirious, because the few words he uttered made no sense to Nancy. He was paler than the day before.

The sun was just visible over the opposite edge of the canyon wall when they began traveling again, hiking along the side of the shallow stream. They descended deeper and deeper into the canyon. They stopped for lunch where the canyon twisted and came to an end. A waterfall, at least a hundred feet high and with two plumes, splashed down the vertical face of the stone cliffs.

"We must go up there," Tasio said, pointing to what appeared to be a forested plateau above the waterfall. "There is a path that leads up, but it will take a long time to climb it."

Tasio was right. Nancy and George walked in single file, while the Tarahumaras took turns carrying the stretcher with Dr. Stone on it. The anthropologist seemed to be sleeping, but Nancy couldn't help worrying.

During a rest break, Tasio appeared at her side with a deep red crystal set in a piece of dark stone. "It's a garnet," Tasio said. "There are many in the stream if you know what to look for." He handed it to her. "It's for you." Then he quickly walked away.

"This probably sounds weird," George said quietly, "but I think he likes you."

"I don't know about that," Nancy replied, and quickly filled George in on her conversation with Tasio. "He seems to want to get us to civilization as soon as possible," she concluded. "I think he wants to be rid of us."

"Well, that's a relief," George said. "I never had the feeling he would hurt us, but . . ." Her words trailed off.

"I know what you mean," Nancy said, standing up. "We could be traveling with a murderer —or two." She gave a deep sigh. "Until Dr. Stone regains consciousness and we can question him, there's not much else we can do." Nancy looked down at the garnet again, then put it in the pocket of her khaki pants.

"Nice little souvenir," George said, standing up and stretching.

Nancy gave a little laugh. "Somehow I don't think I'll need a souvenir to remember this trip."

They were still traveling in late afternoon, climbing slowly up the side of the canyon on a narrow rocky path that meandered back and forth. Nancy could see that Tasio was getting impatient.

They stopped to rest and pass around a bag of

pine nuts once again. "These really work," George said, tossing a handful of the little nuts in her mouth and chewing. "I always get a burst of energy after snacking on them."

"Not that there's much else to eat," Nancy commented.

While the others lay back to grab a few winks, Nancy pushed herself up and walked among the pine trees bordering the path. They were up high enough now to be able to look out over the long canyon, and even though she was exhausted, she wanted to see the view.

She hiked to a cliff and stood looking at the bottom of the canyon, now in shadow. In the semidarkness the canyon was both majestic and mysterious.

Suddenly she heard a deep, throaty growl behind her. She froze, a chill creeping up her spine. Slowly she forced herself to turn around.

She heard another growl, and looking up, found herself staring straight into the yellow eyes of a black puma, hunched forward on a ledge and ready to pounce!

Chapter

Sixteen

NANCY STOOD FROZEN, unable to move.

Suddenly Tasio jumped into the clearing, brandishing a flaming hemp torch. The great black cat arched its back, bristling, and with its head back, roared. Tasio leapt between Nancy and the puma and held the fire in front of the great cat.

"Stay behind me, Nancy," Tasio said quietly.

The puma roared again and twisted its neck. It glanced at them angrily, its long pink tongue darting from between its sharp white fangs. Once again Tasio shouted, shaking the torch but going no closer. Finally the puma jumped to one side. Then it bounded into a copse of trees and disappeared into the shadows.

Tasio turned to Nancy. "Are you all right?"

Nancy still felt frozen with terror. She forced

herself to nod. Tasio hesitated, and then he put his warm arms around her. Nancy let him hug her, aware that she was shaking.

Finally she moved away. "Thank you," she said. "I shouldn't have wandered away like that." She looked at him questioningly. "How did you know where I was?"

"I followed you," he said simply. "I was afraid you'd wander off and get lost. And I brought a torch and matches in case I had to bring you back in the darkness."

"But why didn't you just stop me?"

"I didn't want to take away your freedom," Tasio replied. "I know what that feels like."

Nancy looked away. "Tasio, I'm sorry about distrusting you. I owe you my life."

"So, perhaps Miss Nancy Drew the detective has made a mistake, eh?" Tasio grinned.

"It sometimes happens," Nancy said, her eyes twinkling. "But not very often."

Tasio laughed. He seemed relieved that Nancy was back to her old self. "Pumas are very rare," he told her. "It's too bad you had to run into each other the way you did." He smiled again, and Nancy felt herself smiling back.

"We are almost to our destination," Tasio said. "We will stay the night, and Vitorio will run to a *rancheria* and bring back medical help for Dr. Stone. Tomorrow you and George can go back to your own world."

Oddly, Nancy felt a touch of disappointment. There was something wild and free about being in Copper Canyon, and she felt as if she'd hardly begun to experience it.

Nancy and Tasio walked back to where the others were resting and told the tale of the puma attack. Tasio took great delight in exaggerating the story, while the other Tarahumaras teased him mercilessly.

As they prepared to leave again, George said to Nancy, "I'm worried about Dr. Stone. His breathing is strange, and he hasn't been conscious in hours."

"Tasio told me we'd be able to get him to a doctor by tomorrow morning," Nancy replied.

George still looked worried. "I hope he can last that long."

The final leg of the upward trek seemed to Nancy like the longest stretch yet, but she knew it had to do with her tiredness. Even the Tarahumaras were starting to look beat.

For a while the ground leveled off, then began to rise again, long, smooth slopes that led to a high, forested summit. Celedonio and Patricio led them on a path through a forest.

After a while, Nancy saw the outline of a great ruined wall, almost black against the fading sky. As they moved closer, she saw it was an abandoned mission church. The roof had fallen in, but the thick adobe walls were still standing, draped now with vines and bright orange flowers.

Tasio walked over to her. "There is a room at the back of the church, the sacristy, with a roof and fireplace, and doors to keep out the cold."

"When was this built?" Nancy asked, amazed at stumbling across a huge, ruined building seemingly in the middle of nowhere.

Tasio shrugged. "No one knows how long this church has been here, but certainly for hundreds of years. No one even remembers its name. In our language, we call it the Forgotten Cathedral."

The group walked to the back of the ruined mission church. The sacristy's tile roof was mostly intact, and thick wooden doors had been firmly closed against the elements. Tasio and Celedonio pulled hard. The rusty iron hinges screeched as the door was opened.

The group entered the small room. Nancy looked around. A fireplace with a raised hearth filled one corner, and a narrow door, hanging open, led into the nave. On the other side of the room, a raised stone ledge was covered with straw and baskets.

Chacho and Vitorio quickly carried the stretcher with Dr. Stone on it and placed it carefully on the stone ledge, while Celedonio stacked kindling in the fireplace. Soon they had a warm fire blazing. Chacho began to boil the water that Patricio had carried in from the nearby stream while Tasio and Vitorio left to forage for the wild herbs to make another pot of medicinal brew.

Nancy knelt beside Dr. Stone and pressed her hand to his forehead. It was burning hot. She took his pulse; it seemed weak. His breathing was unsteady.

George brought an earthen pot filled with cool water, dipped a cotton rag into it and pressed it against Dr. Stone's forehead. "It's the only way we can bring down the fever. I'm really worried."

Nancy nodded. "We *have* to get Dr. Stone to civilization tomorrow. If his fever gets any worse, he could die!"

Late that same Wednesday afternoon, less than fifty miles away from the ruined mission, Frank and Joe arrived back in Creel after a four-hour helicopter ride over Copper Canyon with the Westons. On landing, Marcus and Dick Weston had abruptly disappeared in one of the Land Rovers with Sam and Ernie, leaving Cory to drive the Hardys to the hotel.

If the Westons had been upset about Frank and Joe disappearing in the morning, they hadn't shown it.

"Dinner?" Cory Weston invited, parking the Land Rover in front of the hotel.

Frank and Joe exchanged glances. "I don't

know about you guys, but I'm beat," Joe said. "Too tired to eat."

"Me, too," Frank added. As they passed through the hotel lobby, the desk clerk called to him.

"A message for you, señor," he said, holding up an envelope.

Frank took it, surprised to see the return address on the corner.

"Who's it from?" Cory asked.

"It's from our dad," Frank told him, stuffing it into his shirt pocket. "He sent it Express Mail."

Noticing the suspicious look on Cory's face, Joe added quickly, "We called him from here yesterday to let him know where we were."

Before they separated to go to their rooms, Cory said, "I'll phone Colonel Ramirez to see if they've found anything."

Frank nodded. "Thanks. Let us know, okay?"

When the Hardys were finally alone in their room, Joe turned to Frank. "Who's the letter really from?" he asked.

"Detective Garcia," Frank told him, pulling the envelope from his shirt pocket. "Thanks for backing up my story to Cory. I don't want the Westons knowing every move we make."

Frank unfolded the letter and began to read. "What's it say?" Joe asked.

"Garcia wants us to meet him tonight at eight," Frank said.

"Do you think he's found a way for us to get into Tarahumara country?"

Frank shrugged. "More likely, someone's going to check us out first."

Frank and Joe left their room an hour early, grabbing some burritos and lemonade at a stand-up snack bar. Frank showed the proprietor the address in the letter and received directions as well as a small map drawn on a paper napkin.

They made their way up steep, narrow streets. The air was cool and the night sky inky black but blazing with stars. At a long, high adobe wall, wide wooden gates were open, and a long drive wound upward. They could make out the lights of some buildings.

Joaquin Garcia stepped into the light of the street from the wall where he had been standing. He greeted them with a smile.

"My friend is waiting," he said, motioning Frank and Joe to follow him inside the compound. "This is a Jesuit school. Many of the students are Tarahumara Indians."

The school, a series of log and adobe buildings, was set among pine trees. In the center, at the highest point on the hill, was a tall stucco church with a steeple. Garcia led them to a small building with a flat roof next to the church. Warm yellow light burned from a window.

The detective rapped quickly on the stout wooden door. They waited only a moment before it was thrown open. A huge man stood in the doorway. He wore black pants, a black shirt, and a tight, white clerical collar.

"Father Sebastien," Garcia said. "These are the two young men I told you about."

After Garcia introduced the Hardys, the burly priest studied Frank and Joe. Then he backed away from the door, motioning them inside.

The room was simple, with bare adobe walls and high ceilings. Bookcases ran along one wall. A large crucifix hung on another wall. Several stout wooden tables were strewn with magazines, books, and papers, and one held a computer. Three oversize stuffed chairs were grouped around a beehive-shaped fireplace. The room was ablaze with light, and a fire roared in the hearth.

The priest motioned them to sit in wooden chairs around one of the long tables. "You are friends of Dr. Stone?"

"We met Dr. Stone in Tucson," Frank said, "when we met Tasio."

At the mention of the young runner's name, Father Sebastien grunted approvingly. "He could be an Olympic runner, perhaps. Tasio came to this school. Here we try to provide the best education possible, while allowing the young native boys and girls to live traditional lives as well."

"Father Sebastien came here from Montreal more than twenty-five years ago and founded this school," Garcia offered. "And since he is a medical doctor, he founded the hospital, too."

"That is true. But sometimes I'm still not sure what I am doing." Father Sebastien sighed. "It is very difficult for a Tarahumara to be both Indian and Mexican. So they say that our graduates are of both worlds and of neither at the same time. Once they have an education, they want to join the greater world, to become Mexican. Tasio is one of our best pupils, but he is still Tarahumara. He is a prospect for the Mexican Olympic team, yet he remains with his people in a remote village."

"Do you think Tasio killed this man Bernardo Lupe?" Frank asked.

At this the priest's eyes caught fire and his giant eyebrows lowered like storm clouds. "It's impossible," he spat out.

"But they were enemies, weren't they?" Joe asked. "Didn't Tasio swear to stop Lupe from logging even after the Tarahumaras lost in court?"

Father Sebastien put his hands up, as if to stop Joe from saying anything more. "You'll say it's impossible to predict whether or not someone will commit murder, but Tasio had no reason to kill Lupe. Lupe had renounced his logging rights."

Frank noticed an expression of utter surprise cross Garcia's face.

"That's impossible," the detective murmured. Addressing Frank and Joe, he explained, "Lupe fought hard for the rights to sell those logs. He would never give them up."

Father Sebastien stared into the fire. Then he swung around on his seat and faced the others at the table.

"I was Bernardo Lupe's confessor," he told them. "What he told me in the confessional is between him and God. But I can tell you everything else. Bernardo Lupe was dying of cancer. He only had a few weeks left. He was a very successful man, very rich, but he had done terrible things to get his wealth. He was terrified that his eternal soul would go to hell. So he signed papers renouncing the logging rights in Copper Canyon—the same ones he'd fought so hard for in court against the Tarahumara Indians."

Frank gave a low whistle of surprise. "When did he do this?" he asked.

"The morning of the day he was murdered," Father Sebastien said. "Then he brought them to me. He said he was going to Arizona that day, and he asked me to keep the documents safe." The priest shuffled among stacks of paper until he came up with a thick sheaf of legal papers. "Here they are."

Detective Garcia unfolded them and looked them over. "*Sí,* he has renounced all claim to the forest, for himself and for his descendants for all time."

"And he did it two days ago," Joe said, pointing to the date on the line next to Lupe's signature. "The same day he appeared at the Double W." He brightened. "That's what he was arguing with the Westons about, Frank, I'll bet you anything."

Frank nodded. "So the Westons knew that their logging deal was going to fall through."

Father Sebastien looked sharply at the brothers. "The Westons? You know them?"

"We're friends of Marcus Weston's son Cory," Joe explained.

"Bernardo Lupe had a secret partner," Father Sebastien said. "Dr. Stone had reason to believe it was Marcus Weston."

"I think he's right," Joe said. "At least, I saw Bernardo Lupe at their ranch. I recognized him when Garcia showed us the photograph of his body."

"You said Tasio had no reason to kill Lupe because he already knew Lupe was giving up his logging rights," Frank said. "But how did Tasio find out?"

"I met Dr. Stone at his hotel in Chihuahua two nights ago," Father Sebastien explained. "And I told him and Tasio." He brightened. "I met your friends, for only a moment. I'm sure they are well and in no danger. The Tarahumaras can survive most admirably in that wilderness."

"I'd like to know why they took off in the first place," Joe said.

Garcia and the Jesuit priest exchanged looks. Garcia nodded, and Father Sebastien cleared his throat. "Detective Garcia secretly informed me that Tasio Humada's papers had been found at the scene of the crime, and I knew that he was about to be arrested by Colonel Ramirez."

"Colonel Ramirez is very dangerous," Garcia broke in. "He is a corrupt officer, and he will stop at nothing. To him, Tasio Humada and the other Tarahumaras are a nuisance, and he has been known to take justice into his own hands."

"Which means Tasio could have been killed before he ever saw a judge," Father Sebastien concluded. "I made sure some of Tasio's people knew about it. So they stopped the train and got Tasio and your friends out of there."

"Can you take us into Copper Canyon?" Frank asked.

The priest nodded. "Tomorrow morning. We'll leave before dawn. There is a fiesta at a *ranchería* where many Tarahumaras will come to celebrate. It's possible that someone will have word of Tasio and your friends."

"Excellent," Joe said excitedly.

"But I must warn you," Father Sebastien

added, "Copper Canyon is a whole new country. The Tarahumaras are the only Indians in all of North America who were never conquered by invaders, neither Spanish conquistadors nor even the American cavalry. And they have kept their old ways, their old spirits. This part of Copper Canyon is not really even Mexico, but a journey into history."

Father Sebastien's voice faded and he gazed past Frank and Joe to the wooden crucifix across the room. He added softly, "Into a past that has never died."

Chapter

Seventeen

Early Thursday morning Frank and Joe Hardy dressed quietly in their hotel room while it was still dark. They'd agreed to meet Father Sebastien several blocks away, and wanted to leave the hotel before any of the Westons were up.

They crossed the lobby and stepped outside, just in time to see the Weston bodyguards, Sam and Ernie, in front of the hotel. The Land Rover the Westons had been using was idling at the foot of the steps. Frank and Joe ducked back and flattened themselves against the wall of the long porch that ran across the front of the hotel. It was dark there, and they were fully concealed. Then Frank and Joe heard Dick Weston's voice.

"Keep your eyes open for them two snoopy brothers," the young man ordered the two body-guards. "If they go anywhere this morning, I want to know what they're up to." Dick Weston walked toward the Land Rover.

"Looks like the Westons had their own plans this morning, after all," Joe whispered to Frank.

"Come on, Dick." Marcus Weston stuck his head out the window of the Land Rover. "I want to get up in the helicopter before sunrise. I figure if we get an early start, we might catch those Indians unawares and spot them. Especially if they've lit a fire."

"Sure thing, Dad," Dick Weston said, climbing behind the wheel. "I'm just making sure the Hardys don't slip out to investigate." He pro-nounced the last word with heavy sarcasm.

Frank and Joe saw Cory roll down the window by the rear seat, and his voice was clearly audible. "Dick, you act like Frank and Joe are our ene-mies," Cory protested. "They're my friends. And I still don't see why we didn't ask them to join us this morning. I thought we were looking for Nancy and George."

"I'm the one who'll decide who's our enemy and who's not," Dick said. "Me and Dad. And we don't want them with us today. Just in case we find who *we're* looking for. And I don't mean them two girls."

From his hiding place, Frank saw a look of

anger flash across Cory's face. Dick Weston engaged the engine and drove the Land Rover off. The two bodyguards, Sam and Ernie, headed for the second Land Rover, in the parking lot. From it, Frank realized, the two bodyguards would have a clear view of the front steps.

"Quick—into the hotel," Frank said. "Before those goons spot us!"

The Hardys entered the hotel and headed through the restaurant and out the same door they'd used the day before. They made their way to the rendezvous site, at the corner of two streets where a trading post was located. A dented, old Jeep was waiting for them, with Father Sebastien at the wheel.

He greeted them with barely a nod, and as soon as they climbed in, he took off through the small town and onto a road that led into a pine forest. As they drove higher into the mountains, the road began to narrow, until it was barely more than a trail.

"Before we get to the *ranchería,* I must warn you about handshakes," Father Sebastien told them, gripping the wheel firmly as the front tires hit another gaping pothole.

"Handshakes?" Joe asked, puzzled. "What about them?"

"If you shake a Tarahumara's hand firmly—if you squeeze his hand even a little—he will take insult and turn away from you."

"But that's the normal way of shaking hands," Frank pointed out.

The priest chuckled. "In the United States it is, but it's the opposite here. When you squeeze someone's hand too hard, they feel that you are trying to dominate them, and they resent it. In Tarahumara country, when you shake a hand, you must barely touch the other person's palm."

"Maybe that's why the Tarahumara runners were all so shy when we first met them. I remember gripping everyone's hand and giving them a solid shake. No wonder they were kind of distant," Joe said.

"That'll do it," Father Sebastien said jovially. "So now you know. There'll be a lot of people at this festival. The Tarahumaras love to dance, and they use any occasion as an excuse. In fact, a true Tarahumara believes that the only sin in life is not enough dancing."

"What's the occasion this time?" Frank asked.

"A festival giving thanks for the harvest," Father Sebastien said. "It's a very old traditional dance called Rutuburi. Families will come for many miles. Someone, I am certain, will have information about Tasio and your friends."

Not far from where Frank and Joe were, in the mountains of Copper Canyon, Nancy shivered as she sat on the hard ground beneath a great old fir tree. Not far away, Celedonio and Vitorio slept.

Nancy had insisted that she go with them to fetch a doctor for Dr. Stone. After a long talk with the others, Tasio turned to her. "You may go with them, but be careful. Ramirez may have agents among the Tarahumara at the festival. If they spot you, they'll know that I cannot be far behind."

"And I'd hate to think what that creep Ramirez might do to you to get information," George said to Nancy. "Are you sure this is a good idea?"

"She's right." Tasio nodded. "You can still change your mind."

"No," Nancy said. "Dr. Stone is an old friend of my father. I feel obligated to make sure help gets here as quickly as possible." She didn't add that she also wanted Dr. Stone well so she could question him about his mysterious activities the morning they had left Chihuahua.

Nancy had left the Forgotten Cathedral with Celedonio and Vitorio well after dark, and they had traveled continuously. Fortunately, much of the trek was downhill, and the myriad stars in the cold, dark sky had cast enough light for her to see.

When it was almost dawn, Vitorio announced a halt. "There is a *ranchería* nearby. We must wait for sunrise."

Without another word, he pulled his blanket tightly around him and sank to the ground, instantly asleep. Celedonio did likewise. Nancy crouched, tucking the thick wool blanket around her and pulling her head under it. It was better than nothing, but she couldn't seem to get warm. She sat shivering and waiting for what seemed like hours before Celedonio and Vitorio awakened.

After a quick snack of pine nuts, they walked through the forest to a dirt road and open land where sheep were grazing. Ahead in a clearing, Nancy saw a long log house with a shingled roof. Behind it was a row of small log buildings.

They approached to within fifty feet. Celedonio signaled Nancy and Vitorio to stop. Much to Nancy's puzzlement, they sat on a rocky knoll with their backs to the house, even though she knew they could be seen clearly from the house. Nancy waited. No one said a word.

"What are we doing?" Nancy finally asked, glancing back toward the house. Someone in the house was standing at the window, observing them.

"Don't look," Celedonio said. "It's not polite. We must wait until we are invited into the house. It is a Tarahumara custom. If they do not come out to greet us, then we are not wanted."

"How long will it take?" Nancy asked.

"Whenever they are ready," Vitorio said.

Fifteen minutes passed, and Nancy heard the door of the house opening. An old man called to them. Celedonio and Vitorio jumped up and turned around, shouting greetings in reply.

Nancy turned to face the house. A white-haired Tarahumara man, his weathered skin the color of tree bark, slowly made his way from the porch of the log house and across the yard. Celedonio and Vitorio walked over to the old man and spoke to him. Nancy followed.

While they were talking, Nancy saw a young, raven-haired woman appear at the open door of the farmhouse. She wore a brilliant red skirt and a bright yellow blouse. In her arms was a squirming toddler. Two other children peeked out from around her skirts.

For a long moment the old man scrutinized Nancy. Finally he smiled and spoke rapidly.

"He welcomes you to his small farm," Celedonio translated. "And he offers us something to eat."

The old man went back to the house, shooing the woman and children inside, and shutting the door behind him. Celedonio and Vitorio seemed satisfied. Tired of asking questions, Nancy decided to wait this one out. A few minutes later the elderly farmer reemerged. This time an adolescent boy, dressed in the traditional *tagora* and *napatza,* was with him.

The man and boy carried baskets and clay pots. After putting their goods down, they nodded goodbye and returned to their house.

The pot was filled with fresh well water, and there were pine nuts and fresh tamales in corn husks, still warm from the fire. In the other basket, clean and neatly folded, were a colorful yellow *napatza* and a long, white skirt that Vitorio called a *sepucha*.

Vitorio was smiling irresistibly. "Wearing these, perhaps you will not be so obviously spotted if Ramirez has his people about. As for your hair . . ." He picked up a bright red shawl. "You can cover your head with this."

Nancy took the basket of clothing and walked into the woods to change. Although the colors were garish, the skirt and blouse were beautiful, and she was glad to finally have a change of clothing. She took off her T-shirt and decided to leave it behind. The blouse would do until she got back to civilization. She decided to leave her khaki pants on under the skirt, however, and she carefully rolled them up. Although the skirt was loose-fitting, she wanted to be able to get rid of it if it got in the way of hiking through the woods. She pushed her reddish blond hair away from her face and covered it with the red shawl. Under close scrutiny, Nancy knew, she stood no chance of passing as a Tarahumara woman. But from a distance, she could at least blend in with a crowd.

When she reappeared, she noticed that even

the normally serious Celedonio was unable to stop smiling.

"It's a disguise, silly," Nancy admonished him, feeling slightly resentful.

"I am sorry," Celedonio said. "But you look beautiful dressed as a Tarahumara woman."

When she saw Vitorio nodding in agreement, Nancy blushed. "Come on," she said quickly. "We have to get to a doctor."

They followed a rutted gravel road beside a stream for almost an hour until they came to a bluff overlooking a wide valley of farmland framed by forests of pine. Below, Nancy saw a sprawling wooden house. Several small houses stood nearby, with ancient arching willows between them. A row of smaller storehouses stood behind the main house.

Nancy could see dozens of Indian people in brightly colored clothing milling about in front of the big house. More people squatted around fires, near large tents. She could hear fiddle music, the unrelenting beat of drums, and chanting. As if rising up from the soil, a circle of Tarahumara Indians in the middle of the throng moved to the primal beat.

"Come!" Vitorio said eagerly. "Finally we shall feast."

Celedonio laughed. "Enough of these pine nuts."

Nancy looked at them, surprised. "You mean, you can't stand them, either?"

"Not after eating nothing else for days," Celedonio said, flashing a smile.

Nancy laughed. She pulled the bright red shawl tightly over her head and around the lower part of her face.

As they approached the farmhouse, they passed other Indians walking up the road. No one seemed to take any particular notice of Nancy or the two Taras with her. Indians sat in small groups making music or feeding children, and teenage boys in white *tagoras* and red *napatzas* watched other boys wrestling in the mud. Wooden platters and clay pots had been filled with food and set out, and a small group of men spooned drinks into clay mugs from a giant vat.

"We must find the owner of this *ranchería*," Celedonio explained to Nancy. He steered her and Vitorio around the throng, and they edged around the side of the big wooden house. Suddenly Nancy froze. Twenty feet away, striding through the gate from the road, was the priest from the hotel in Chihuahua—Father Sebastien!

She was about to warn Celedonio when the Jesuit moved to one side, and Nancy was even more astonished. Frank and Joe Hardy were walking right behind him!

Chapter

Eighteen

Do not let them see you yet," Celedonio warned, standing in front of Nancy to block her from view.

Of course, she realized. It could be dangerous to make a scene. Silently she followed Celedonio and Vitorio around the back of the house, near the storehouses, where there were no people. Vitorio disappeared but was soon back, with Father Sebastien and the Hardys.

Frank flung his arms around Nancy when he finally recognized who was standing in the full skirt, yellow blouse, and bright red shawl.

"I'm so glad to see you and Joe," Nancy said, hugging Frank back.

He couldn't resist teasing her. "You'll start a new fashion sensation back home," he said.

Nancy ignored Frank's teasing. She was more concerned about why Joe and Frank were with the Jesuit. But before she could say anything, Joe asked, "Where's George?"

"She's with Dr. Stone in the mountains, at a place called the Forgotten Cathedral. He's badly hurt. He needs a doctor. Maybe even a helicopter evacuation."

Celedonio acted alarmed. "But to get a helicopter is impossible without the police finding out. And if Tasio falls into Ramirez's hands, he might be killed."

Father Sebastien raised his hand to quiet him. "But I am a medical doctor. You can take me to Dr. Stone, and Tasio will remain safe."

"Yes, of course." Celedonio turned to Nancy. "Father Sebastien is the man who sent us word that Colonel Ramirez would arrest Tasio on the train."

"*Sí,*" Vitorio affirmed. "He has helped our people for many years."

"I do what I can," Father Sebastien murmured, almost apologetically. "Of course, it has been helpful to have friends who are high-level functionaries. Even when they are corrupt." His eyes twinkled. "*Especially* when they are corrupt," he added.

Nancy eyed the priest carefully. "The night we were introduced at the hotel, you were arguing with Dr. Stone," she reminded him.

"Ah, yes," Father Sebastien said. "Much has transpired. I have told some of it to your friends."

Frank brought Nancy up to date on the murder of Bernardo Lupe and the evidence—or lack of it—against Tasio.

Nancy was relieved. If Tasio didn't have a motive to kill Bernardo Lupe—and if Lupe had renounced the logging claims, Tasio didn't have a motive—then he could certainly be moved down on the list of suspects, if not off it altogether.

"That night, I brought news of this to Dr. Stone and Tasio," Father Sebastien said. "Dr. Stone refused to believe it, of course.

"It seemed impossible to Dr. Stone that someone could give up something he had fought so hard for, because he wanted to make peace with his soul." The priest looked earnestly at Nancy. "When you overheard us arguing, it was because Bingham Stone didn't trust Lupe to keep his promise."

"So if Tasio didn't kill Lupe," Nancy demanded, "who did?"

"It is not for me to accuse," said Father Sebastien. "I have my suspicions, but for now my main concern must be Dr. Stone. I will retrieve my bag from the Jeep, and we shall depart."

Celedonio, Vitorio, and Father Sebastien left, while Nancy, Frank, and Joe remained by the row of storehouses. Father Sebastien returned first, then Celedonio with a basket of food and a jug of water. Vitorio returned last, bearing ominous news. "There are men circulating in the crowd asking if anyone has word of Tasio Humada and the *chabochis*—the gringos—he ran off with into the mountains."

"Ramirez's people. We must go quickly," Celedonio announced. He lifted the basket of food, slinging it onto his back and tying the straps around his chest.

Nancy decided she was simply too tired to feel tired—a strange state of exhaustion. They retraced their journey of the night before.

She noticed that despite his size, Father Sebastien strode through the wilderness with surprising alacrity, at times outpacing even Frank and Joe. He hiked with a sense of purpose and refused to let any of the others carry his heavy black bag.

They arrived on a bluff of rocks overlooking the Forgotten Cathedral by midafternoon. Nancy was weary, and every muscle in her body ached. Celedonio took Nancy's red shawl and waved it. In response, down in the gaping doorway of the ruined building, someone waved a tiny white flag.

Half an hour later they reached the church. Chacho and Patricio raced out to greet them. Tasio remained behind, a worried expression on his face.

"Dr. Stone is in the sacristy?" Father Sebastien

asked. Tasio nodded. Without stopping, the priest walked to the back of the church and disappeared inside. Tasio approached Nancy.

"George is with Bing. His fever is very high, so she gives him a sponge bath with cold water from the river. But I am afraid it is too late." His next words were barely audible. "Because of me, he will die."

Nancy reached out and clasped Tasio's hand. "It's not your fault," she said. "You did your duty to your people by fighting for their rights, and because of that, you're in this terrible mess. But Dr. Stone is your friend, and when you're someone's friend, you have to stand up for their rights—even if that means suffering for it."

"I know you are trying to make me feel better. But if Bing dies," he added softly, "I will never forgive myself."

Patricio and several other Tarahumaras prepared a dinner from the food they had brought back from the *ranchería,* and they ate it in the ruins of the old church while Father Sebastien ministered to Bingham Stone. Finally the priest joined them.

"Dr. Stone has a serious infection in the wound in his head, and I am concerned it has spread to his brain," he told them. "I have given him an injection of an antibiotic. We must take turns watching him tonight. But if all goes well, his fever will break and he will be fine."

The Tarahumaras were quiet, as were Nancy, George, and the Hardys. The physical toll of the past few days was evident in their tired expressions. Finally, Father Sebastien broke the silence.

"Undoubtedly you saved your life by fleeing the train, Tasio. And I believe you are innocent of the murder of Bernardo Lupe. But this"—the priest gestured to the canyon and the ruined adobe church—"is not a solution, to hide in these mountains. If you want justice, you must go to Creel and demand it."

The Jesuit's speech instantly grabbed everyone's attention. Tasio's expression was impassive, but Celedonio exploded. "If he goes into Creel, Colonel Ramirez will take him prisoner immediately. And then—*phhhtt!*" Celedonio made a motion with his hand, as if something were going up in smoke. "Tasio will be dead."

"Perhaps not," the priest said. "The priests in my order will support Tasio, and there is another officer in Creel who will do everything he can to ensure that Tasio has a fair trial. His name is Joaquin Garcia, and today he has gone to Chihuahua to seek help from other honest police. Ramirez is powerful, but he is not invincible. You must face justice, Tasio. And you must trust in the Great Spirit that you will win."

Nancy saw a troubled expression pass over Tasio's face. "And how will justice help my people?" he asked bitterly. "What if I am thrown into jail for the rest of my life for a crime I did not commit?"

The Jesuit rose and walked over to Tasio. He placed his hand on the youth's shoulder. "And if you live the rest of your life as a fugitive? As a wild Tarahumara haunting the most remote *barranca* of Copper Canyon?" His voice rose until he was almost shouting. "You will throw away your life, and your people will have nothing. Ramirez is a Goliath. Tasio must be David, and Tasio must slay him with the truth."

Another heavy silence fell over the gathering. Tasio seemed to be deep in thought. Finally he nodded. "Father Sebastien, I will do this, because it is your wish."

The priest patted him on the shoulder again. "I thank you, Tasio." He turned to the other Indians and called out. "Patricio, Chacho. You must leave immediately for Creel and locate a detective named Joaquin Garcia." He described the police officer. "You will tell him that Tasio is prepared to surrender but that it will only be done through my intercession." He paused, then added, "And be very careful. All our lives will be in jeopardy if you are caught."

A few minutes later the two runners were off to Creel. The Jesuit asked for a few hours to sleep and pray, while someone watched over Bingham Stone. Frank and Joe insisted on taking the first two shifts. Nancy was so tired that she could barely move. She dragged herself off to one of the straw mounds in the sacristy and wrapped herself in a wool blanket. Before she knew it, she was dead to the world.

She awoke to the sounds of several other people breathing nearby and a shaft of daylight lying across her face from the open door. Nancy threw back her blanket and looked around. She made out George's sleeping form in the half-light. Joe was sitting quietly beside Dr. Stone. Nancy realized that no one had awakened her during the night to take her turn.

As if reading her thoughts, Joe said, "You were sleeping too soundly—I didn't want to disturb you. Dr. Stone's fever broke a few hours ago, and he regained consciousness for a few minutes. I think he's going to be all right."

Father Sebastien walked in then with Frank, who carried a clay pot filled with water. "Yes, Dr. Stone will be fine," he confirmed, "although a few days in a hospital bed are warranted. If all goes well, Joaquin Garcia will be here with a contingent of his men by noon."

Although Nancy knew Tasio was making the best decision, it also frightened her. Tasio would be led away in handcuffs and forced to prove his innocence in a court of law. There were no guarantees, Nancy knew. She also knew that once they were back in Creel, she wouldn't rest until she found the real murderer. She was sure that George, Frank, and Joe would join her.

Frank took the pot of water to the side of Bingham Stone's bed, and the priest began to sponge the patient's forehead. Nancy walked outside and strolled down to the stream, where she splashed ice-cold mountain water on her face and arms. She found herself wishing for a hot shower. After running her fingers through her shoulder-length hair in an attempt to get the tangles out, she returned to the sacristy.

"Dr. Stone is conscious," Joe told Nancy quietly as she approached.

Nancy rushed inside and saw Father Sebastien chortling over a joke he had just shared with Bingham Stone. The anthropologist was propped up on blankets that had been folded into a pillow shape. He was pale, but his eyes were clear and focused.

"I have told my old friend what has happened in the last few days," Father Sebastien said to Nancy and the Hardys.

Bingham Stone gazed at the three young sleuths and began to speak, his voice thin but firm. "When Father Sebastien told me Bernardo Lupe had surrendered the logging rights he'd fought so hard for, I didn't believe it," he said, shaking his head in disbelief.

"And, anyway, that night in Chihuahua, I

wanted to know who Lupe's partner was. I long suspected it was Marcus Weston. The Weston family is well known in Arizona. I knew they owned a lumber mill, and a year ago I spotted Marcus Weston here in Creel with Bernardo Lupe. So even if Lupe stopped clear-cutting the forests on Tarahumara land, there were no guarantees Weston or another crook with lots of money to bribe government officials wouldn't step in and grab the logging rights for himself."

"Why don't you relax, Dr. Stone," George suggested. The older man was clearly pushing his scarce energy reserves to talk. "You can tell us the rest of the story later."

Stone raised a trembling hand. "No, no, I must tell you now. I took a taxi from our hotel in Chihuahua to Lupe's ranch. I figured I'd have my own talk with him to see if he really meant what he said. When I got there, a Land Rover was parked in the drive, and several men were standing outside Lupe's house. I crept as close to the house as I could, hiding behind trees. The drive was well lit, and I saw everyone's face clearly. Some I knew."

Dr. Stone's voice faltered. Frank helped him drink more water. Then Stone resumed his tale. "They were shouting at Bernardo Lupe, and he was very quiet. Then the men stormed away and got in the car. Except for one person. He pulled a gun from his pocket, turned, and shot Lupe."

"Who was it?" Joe and Nancy asked simultaneously.

Bingham Stone paused a moment. Then he said, "I recognized Marcus Weston and Colonel Ramirez. But it was a young man who pulled the trigger. Afterward, Marcus Weston called out to him."

"Dick Weston," Frank said.

Stone nodded. "Dick. That was it. That was the name Marcus Weston used. And I know that Marcus Weston has a son named Dick."

There was a stunned silence in the room. Frank spoke first. "It makes sense. Dick Weston kills Lupe for double-crossing the Weston family. To Dick, Lupe became a traitor when he renounced those logging rights. And his father and Ramirez are now trying to protect him."

"By framing Tasio, they can get Dick off the hook and get Tasio off their backs," Joe said.

"I saw Colonel Ramirez throw something on the ground and stomp on it," Dr. Stone said. "It must have been Tasio's identification papers."

Tasio nodded. "Stolen that day in Chihuahua."

"Probably by one of Ramirez's own agents," George speculated. "I'll bet he and Dick decided to kill Lupe long before they paid him a visit that night. So they arranged to steal Tasio's papers and frame him."

"It's great to have Lupe's murder all figured

out, but what about physical evidence?" Nancy asked. "In court, Dr. Stone's testimony might not be believed since he's a friend of Tasio. We still need physical evidence to tie the Westons to Lupe's murder, and we don't have any."

"Oh, but we do," Bingham Stone said matter-of-factly. He dropped his bombshell. "Before leaving the hotel in Chihuahua, I borrowed George's camera."

"You mean it wasn't stolen!" George exclaimed.

"Not at all," Dr. Stone said calmly. "Although you did leave it right on your bed where any thief could find it. And it had a roll of film already in it. So I borrowed it. I did mean to ask permission, but I couldn't find you."

Nancy looked at George. "We were making that phone call to Frank and Joe at the Double W."

Dr. Stone continued. "And from my hiding place at Lupe's hacienda, I was able to photograph the arrival of the Westons and Ramirez, and even the murder itself, when Dick Weston fired the gun." Stone's voice faltered, as if what he remembered sickened him.

"But it was night," Joe pointed out. "If you didn't use a flash, it wouldn't have turned out."

"There were four powerful halogen spotlights mounted on the roof of Weston's Land Rover," Bingham Stone said. "So it was very bright. And

I lowered the camera's shutter speed so more light could reach the film. I'm a bit of a camera buff, and I'm pretty sure I got a good picture. But I knew I couldn't go to the police until I had the film developed. I needed concrete proof."

"Where's the camera now?" George asked.

"In my canvas shoulder bag," Stone said. "I had it when I got to the train, I'm sure of it."

Nancy looked at George. "We didn't bring any luggage. We had to leave it all behind."

"That means it's fallen into Ramirez's hands," George said angrily.

"Just one second," Joe said, looking at Frank. "You remember a canvas shoulder bag?"

Frank nodded. "We retrieved the luggage from the Creel police station. The canvas bag, and presumably the camera with the photographs of the murder, are in our hotel room in Creel!"

The wooden door of the sacristy burst open then, and Vitorio stood in a shaft of brilliant morning light, with a second Tarahumara beside him. The newcomer was a stranger. Vitorio spoke quickly to Tasio. When he was finished, Father Sebastien turned to Nancy and the Hardys.

"This runner has brought terrible news. We are in great danger!" he said. "Police helicopters are searching the neighboring canyon and will soon be flying over the Forgotten Cathedral, too!"

Chapter

Nineteen

THERE WAS A MOMENT of stunned silence. George spoke first. "Maybe it's Joaquin Garcia," she suggested.

The Jesuit sighed and shook his head weakly. "Too soon for the runners to have reached him," he said. "They have probably gotten to Creel by now, but I don't think enough time has passed for them to find Garcia and for Garcia to get all the way back here—even by helicopter."

"Ramirez," Tasio said grimly.

"If we stay in here, maybe they'll fly over without seeing us," George ventured.

"This will be the first place they'll search," the Jesuit replied. "It's the only shelter within miles."

"We'll be cornered if we stay here," Frank said.

"But Dr. Stone is still far too weak to be moved," Nancy protested.

"Nonsense!" the doctor spluttered.

"It's nonsense to think you can go anywhere except a hospital," Nancy retorted in a firm tone.

"Then leave me here," Stone said, his thin voice showing traces of anger. "You go, all of you! Tasio must not fall into Ramirez's hands!"

"I will not go," Tasio announced. "Not if we must leave you for Ramirez to find."

"But with helicopters flying overhead, how *can* we move?" Joe asked. "We'll be spotted."

"Then let's do the opposite," Frank proposed. "Let's be obvious."

Seeing the surprised looks on Joe's and Nancy's faces, Frank said, "It can work. We can create a diversion. There are some pretty good runners here. Let's split into smaller groups and head in different directions. When the helicopters fly over this canyon—"

"Some of us can accidentally-on-purpose be seen!" Nancy finished for him. "And take Ramirez on a wild-goose chase."

Frank nodded. "Ramirez will come after us, but at least we'll lead them away from the church."

"They'll still probably search this place," Joe said, "and find Dr. Stone."

"There are caves nearby," Vitorio interjected, looking at Tasio.

Tasio's eyes lit up. "Yes! With the stretcher, we could carry Bing there before the helicopters arrive."

"We must hurry!" Dr. Stone said. He started pushing the blanket away.

"Let's do it!" Frank walked across the small room and quickly unfolded the stretcher.

When Dr. Stone was on the stretcher, Frank and Vitorio carried him outside. Tasio pointed down the valley. "Some should go that way," he said. "The rest can come with me when I take Bing to the cave. Then we can pass through the forest until we are far enough away from the cave and come out in the open on that cliff."

He pointed to a limestone promontory at the other end of the canyon. It was as high as a six-story building.

"Shhh," Joe suddenly cautioned, raising a finger in warning. "Listen!"

Everyone was silent, straining to hear. Very faintly, Nancy could just make out the steady drone of an engine.

"We must hurry!" Father Sebastien urged.

"I'll go with Tasio," Joe announced. He looked at George. "You should come with us, since we're all runners."

"Good idea," Frank said. "And Nancy will come with me."

"Vitorio will also go with you," Tasio said. "Follow the stream until you come to a path that leads up the side of the canyon. The path is in the open, so you will certainly attract attention."

"What if they start shooting at us?" Nancy asked.

"Then we run for cover as fast as we can," Frank said. "Besides, if they shoot from a helicopter in midair, their aim won't be all that great."

Tasio nodded. "And there are plenty of boulders and trees to hide behind."

Frank and Nancy disappeared with Vitorio, while Joe and Tasio shouldered the stretcher, followed by George, Father Sebastien, and Celedonio. They crossed the chilly stream at a point where the water was only ankle deep and headed up a gravel slope. Already the sound of the helicopters was growing, and soon Joe heard the distinctive *whop-whop whop* of the rotors.

At the top of the gravel slope, they entered a forest of small oak trees. On the far side another cliff rose hundreds of feet straight up to the canyon rim. The stony face was pocked with caves.

Most of them, Joe noticed, were completely inaccessible, since the entrances were dozens of feet above the ground. Soon, however, Tasio stopped at the base of the cliff, near a pile of rocks.

The helicopters' noise was growing louder, reverberating against the stone cliffs of the canyon. Joe glanced back over his shoulder and swallowed.

A helicopter, black against the bright sunlight, rose like a great vulture over the crest of mountains on the other side of the canyon. Almost immediately it was followed by a second one. The choppers hovered for several seconds, as if deciding what to do. Then Joe saw them descend into the valley and head toward the ruined mission.

"Hurry!" Tasio urged. "The cave is here!"

At the top of the pile of rocks, the ground dipped sharply and the cliff wall angled inward. Tasio led them down into a narrow, cool cleft. Ahead of them was the opening of a tunnel. Tasio and Joe carried the stretcher into the cave and set it down not far from the entrance. Joe looked around. In the dim light that filtered in from outside, it was apparent that the cave had been used for shelter before, but not for a long time. Clay pots of different sizes and shapes were piled on one side, but many were broken or overturned. There were no baskets or blankets.

"We dare not light a torch," Father Sebastien said. "Even the smallest bit of smoke might give our hiding place away."

He set the jug of drinking water down next to Dr. Stone.

George's face was drawn with worry. "Are you sure you'll be all right?" she asked.

Dr. Stone fluttered his hand weakly. "Of course. Now go, all of you," he said in a tremulous voice.

Joe looked at Tasio. "Why don't you stay here with Dr. Stone and Father Sebastien? George and I can lead the chopper away."

Tasio shook his head emphatically. "If you wish, you may fight my struggle with me. But not *for* me. I must go, too." He turned to Celedonio, and they spoke in their native tongue. Then he turned back to Joe and George.

"Celedonio will stay in case they have to send someone for help." Tasio started for the entrance to the cave. "Hurry, we must go!"

Joe and George hurried after the Tarahumara leader. They climbed out of the cave, pausing momentarily to scan the floor of the canyon before leaving cover. Joe spotted the helicopters at the ruined mission. One still hovered in the air. The other had landed, although the rotor still revolved, whipping the grass and shrubs into a frenzy with the circular windstream. Several men in police uniforms ran from the old sacristy toward the helicopter. One of the uniforms was decorated with gold braid.

"Ramirez," Joe hissed. In the distance he saw Ramirez crouch and hold his peaked hat as he ran to the side of the chopper. The colonel jumped inside with the two other *federales* right behind him. The rotor began to pick up. The second helicopter, hovering nearby, slowly moved down the valley, following the stream in the direction Frank and Nancy had gone.

"This way!" Tasio urged, waving Joe and George after him. They raced along a trail that led through a small forest of scrub oak trees. Gradually the ground rose and became rockier. The trail was so steep Joe had to grab on to saplings to pull himself up, often ducking to avoid the rocks and pebbles that rolled downhill in George and Tasio's wake.

At one point he looked up and nearly panicked. Tasio and George were gone! Then he saw George peeking down at him over a cliff.

"Hurry," she urged. "There's a plateau up here. And one of the helicopters is headed this way."

Joe doubled his pace. Tasio appeared beside George and extended his arm. Joe grabbed it and pulled himself up over the cliff.

The plateau held a commanding view of the canyon and the mission. Joe saw one helicopter far down the canyon. The second one, rising above the ruined church, was pointed in their direction.

"We must cross." Tasio pointed to the far end of the plateau, several hundred yards away, where another forest of scrub oak began. Their movement would be clearly visible to the helicopter.

"Let's sprint," Joe proposed.

The three runners raced across the plateau. The sound of the helicopter grew steadily louder. When they were halfway across the plateau, Joe glanced to his side—and immediately wished he hadn't. The helicopter was barely fifty feet off the side of the plateau and coming straight toward them.

They had at least five hundred feet to go before they reached the cover of trees. Adrenaline pumping, Joe found a last spurt of speed. The sound of the helicopter was deafening as a great, dark shadow floated over the ground, swallowing the three runners.

The helicopter hovered just ahead of them, veering at an angle to block their progress. The powerful wind from the rotor blew fine bits of dirt into the air, pinging against Joe's skin and forcing him to squint. Suddenly the ground exploded barely ten feet away.

"They're shooting at us!" Joe cried.

"This way!" George shouted. Joe saw her running toward the cliff in an attempt to pass the chopper, with Tasio not far behind her. He heard several more loud popping sounds. The ground around George erupted in a flurry of rocks and pebbles.

Joe watched in horror as George collapsed on the ground!

Chapter

Twenty

JOE AND TASIO ran to George and crouched beside her slumped body.

"George . . . are you all right?" Joe asked anxiously, speaking loudly over the roar of the helicopter. The aircraft had settled to the ground barely fifty feet away.

George nodded. "I lost my balance and fell because of all those rocks flying around me." She pushed herself up. "For a minute I thought I was hit by a bullet, but it must have been the pebbles." She looked over and saw the helicopter. "And now I've ruined things for everyone."

"Don't worry," Joe said, trying to sound reassuring as he and Tasio helped her to her feet. "We've gotten out of tight spots before."

But this time our luck may have run out, he thought.

The door of the helicopter slid open, and several uniformed *federales* leapt out, brandishing rifles. The helicopter's engine died, and as the rotor began to slow, Colonel Ramirez stepped out, his gold braid glittering in the sunlight.

Joe watched Ramirez cup his hand over his brow and peer down the valley. The second helicopter lifted up from the floor of the canyon and headed in their direction. Then Ramirez turned and walked toward Joe, George, and Tasio, a cruel smile on his face. His men closed in from behind, pointing their rifles at the trio.

"Tasio Humada, we have been looking for you for many days," the corrupt colonel said. He glanced coolly at Joe and George. "As for you two, it's most regrettable that you chose to be involved in this business." He gestured down the length of the canyon. The second helicopter was rapidly approaching. "We have captured your friends as well, and they will be here shortly. Then we will decide what to do with you."

A minute later the other chopper settled onto the plateau. To Joe's amazement, Marcus Weston stepped out. Then Nancy and Frank appeared in the entrance, their arms tied behind their backs. Dick Weston stood behind them, prodding them forward with the barrel of his rifle. Nancy and

Frank stumbled from the chopper, barely able to keep their balance with their arms tied. Dick Weston herded them over to stand beside Joe and George, then backed away.

"Where is Vitorio?" Tasio asked in a whisper, without moving his lips.

"He got away," Frank quietly responded.

"Shut up!" Dick Weston yelled at them. Marcus Weston and the colonel huddled together, deep in conversation. Then they broke apart and approached their prisoners. Ramirez's face was dark and cruel. Marcus Weston looked as he always did—jovial and friendly, but his words were ominous.

"More's the pity—you boys had to get involved. Cory will miss his new friends."

"Not that he'll ever know what happened to any of you." Dick Weston sneered at them.

"We know who killed Bernardo Lupe!" Frank shouted at them.

"So do we!" Dick Weston laughed. He jabbed the barrel of his rifle in Tasio's direction. "The Indian over there."

Frank shook his head. "It was you, Dick. And we have proof!"

Ramirez smiled. "The only proof was Tasio Humada's identification papers found on the ground near the body." He laughed. "Of course, as you might have guessed, one of my agents stole them from him in Chihuahua."

"And then he followed us," Nancy said.

Ramirez nodded. "He saw you talking with Tasio and his friend and decided to see what you were up to. I must compliment you on losing him. He is skilled at trailing people and not easily gotten rid of."

"If you guys hadn't been so nosy we wouldn't have to get rid of you now," Dick Weston said.

"What do you mean?" Frank demanded.

"I was listening in on an extension when Nancy Drew phoned you at the hacienda," Dick replied. "Even then, you guys knew too much for my comfort. Now you're going to pay for it."

"Those threatening letters to Tasio," Joe said. "You sent them, didn't you?"

"You bet I did," Dick admitted proudly.

"And you were behind those 'accidents' at the marathon, weren't you?" Nancy accused. "You almost killed your own brother instead." She noticed anger cross Marcus Weston's face as she spoke.

"Yeah, I was driving that car at the shopping mall, and I almost got Tasio then," Dick confessed. "When I missed, I waited at the edge of the cliff near the finish line until I saw Tasio come over the hill. Then I pushed that boulder off. Too bad Cory got in the way."

Dick Weston glanced at his dad. "I didn't even know he was running in the marathon. I was trying to get rid of Tasio Humada, not my brother."

"I didn't approve any of it," Marcus Weston roared angrily at his son.

"But you were there when Dick shot and killed Bernardo Lupe," Joe shot back. "And then you tried to hide it by framing Tasio."

"Lupe was a traitor," Dick Weston said in a thin, mean voice. "He deserved to die."

"He promised us a steady supply of cheap wood for our lumber mill," Marcus Weston interjected. "We gave him the money to bribe officials so we could cut trees on Tarahumara land. Then Tasio Humada started organizing to stop us."

"So we had to get rid of Tasio," Dick finished. He turned, raised his rifle, and pointed it directly at Tasio. "Yeah, I killed Lupe when he wanted to back out of the deal. He deserved it, and so does Tasio."

"Wait!" Ramirez raised his hand. He pointed to Tasio. "We need him to stand trial. When he is convicted, he will rot in prison for the rest of his life, a reminder to all his people of what happens if they stand in our way."

Ramirez turned to face Nancy, Frank, Joe, and George. "These are the ones we do not need. We cannot allow them to give witness. They must be killed."

Nancy saw a look of growing shock on Marcus Weston's face. "You mean——"

"It's too late to be weak about it," Dick Weston interrupted. "Ramirez is right. We have to get rid of them and take Tasio back."

"Often people disappear in the wilderness of Copper Canyon, and they are never seen again," Ramirez continued. "Of course, we will mount a search, but we will also know where not to look." He strode to the edge of the plateau and peered over. "This cliff will be perfect."

"Are all you Westons murderers?" Joe asked.

Dick snorted. "Cory doesn't have the guts. He's totally out to lunch about all this."

"You mean he's innocent," Nancy concluded.

"Call it what you like," Dick told her.

"Tie Tasio Humada up," Ramirez ordered.

One of the officers moved forward to carry out the colonel's order. Ramirez turned to the other man. "The others can start walking—backward, straight toward the edge of this cliff. The fall will kill them instantly."

"No, do not do this!" Tasio shouted. "I will plead guilty of the murder and go to jail if you spare their lives!"

Ramirez chuckled. "So noble of you, Tasio. But I'm afraid it's too late for that."

"Let's go," Dick ordered. He prodded Frank with the barrel of his rifle. "Start walking!"

Slowly the four friends stepped backward. Frank glanced around, desperately trying to think of a last-ditch escape.

"Faster!" Dick shouted.

Frank, Nancy, Joe, and George took another step back. Nancy glanced over her shoulder. The edge of the cliff was only ten feet away. Ramirez stood to one side, right on the brink, waiting for them to plummet to their deaths on the sharp rocks sixty feet below.

Suddenly Nancy heard a shot. One of Ramirez's men screamed, and his rifle flew from his hand. Blood poured down his arm. Dick Weston swung around and started firing wildly at the rocks on the other side of the plateau. The bullets pinged and ricocheted. Another shot rang out. This time Dick Weston flew backward. He sprawled on the ground holding his shoulder, his face contorted with pain.

Frank saw uniformed men and Tarahumaras racing across the plateau. There were more than he could count. Vitorio was among them. Then, to his surprise, he recognized Cory Weston and Joaquin Garcia running from the forest.

From the corner of his eye Frank saw Ramirez pull his revolver from the holster at his waist. "Watch out!" Frank shouted.

Ramirez raised the gun and aimed at Garcia. Joe saw his chance. He spun around and was about to rush the corrupt official when he heard something whistle through the air beside him. There was a sickening thud, and an arrow suddenly sprouted from Ramirez's gun hand.

The colonel screamed in pain and tottered precariously at the edge of the cliff. He dropped his gun, and it fell over the edge.

"Watch out!" Joe shouted.

It was too late. Ramirez toppled backward, his scream fading as he fell.

Chapter
Twenty-One

A DAY LATER Nancy and George stood on the veranda of the Creel Lodge. Bingham Stone sat in a chair nearby, his head swathed in a bandage.

Dr. Stone sniffed the air. "The first blizzards will be coming soon. I'll be glad to get back to Tucson. It's a little warmer there in winter."

"And I'll be glad to get back to River Heights," George said. "This has turned out to be the craziest marathon I ever ran."

"Hopefully not the last," Nancy challenged.

George looked as if her best friend had just said something preposterous. "Of course not! After this one, all the rest will be easy!"

The door of the inn opened, and Frank and Cory emerged, with Joe behind them. Joe had his arm around Rita's shoulders, and they were talking quietly.

"I'm sure glad you flew down from the Double W," he said quietly. "After what we went through, you were just what I needed."

Rita smiled shyly. "When Cory phoned to tell me what had happened, I had to come. We are like brother and sister. I couldn't let Cory face this alone." She smiled again. "Or you, either."

Cory Weston hobbled out of the hotel on his crutches. He had retreated to his room when they returned to Creel, so none of them had spoken to him. Cory looked better than he had the day before, Nancy thought, but he still was grim. It was natural, she knew, considering the terrible events that had transpired.

"We owe you our lives," Nancy said to him. "And we can never repay—"

Cory held up a hand. "That's enough," he said, cutting her off. He set down his crutches and dropped into the chair next to Dr. Stone's. "Look, I only did what was right. The day before yesterday, when we drove out to the helicopter, Colonel Ramirez was waiting for Dick and my dad. I overheard Dick and the colonel talking and found out who Lupe's real murderer was— and why they were trying to frame Tasio."

"Still, it was brave of you to go to Garcia," Joe said, "when you knew your own family was involved."

"I'm ashamed to say it took me twenty-four hours to do it," Cory said. "After I realized what was going on, all I knew was that I couldn't go with Dick and my dad on the search. So I told them I wasn't feeling well, and I drove back to the inn." He paused and looked away.

Watching Cory, Nancy's heart went out to him. It was clear how difficult it had been for him to do the right thing.

"When I got back to the inn, I looked for you," he said to Frank and Joe, "but you were gone. I didn't know what to do. I waited all day for you to come back."

"We were already in Copper Canyon," Frank said.

"I figured you had found a way to get to Nancy and George," Cory said. "That night when my dad and Dick came back and found you gone, they were furious. I knew, then, that if I didn't do something . . ." His voice faded.

George reached out and touched Cory's shoulder. "But you *did* do something, and that's what counts," George said softly.

"Yes," Cory said, struggling to control his emotions. "I knew that Ramirez was sending out a chopper the next morning, and my dad and Dick would be in another. They were closing in on you. I *had* to do something." He paused, then continued softly. "So as soon as Dick and my dad left, I went straight to the police station. Luckily,

I was directed to Detective Garcia. I told him my story. Barely ten minutes later Chacho and Patricio arrived and told us where you guys were hiding."

"You saved our lives," George told Cory, gazing at him fondly.

"My dad always taught me to be proud of the Weston name," Cory said. "Now I'm ashamed of it because of my father's and brother's actions. But I hope what I did makes up for it—just a little."

"You bet it does," Frank said. "You really measured up to your ancestor's standards—I bet Willie Weston would have been proud of you."

Just then a police car slowed to a stop in front of the hotel. Joaquin Garcia, Tasio, and Father Sebastien got out. They climbed the steps to the veranda.

"Tasio has been completely cleared of all charges against him," the Jesuit announced.

"Bravo," Joe cheered.

Tasio stepped toward Nancy and gazed at her with warm, brown eyes. "I don't blame you for not trusting me completely," he said quietly. "Bing and I gave you much to wonder about." He laughed.

Nancy nodded. "You sure did. And as much as I didn't want to believe either of you were murderers, I couldn't rule out the possibility."

Tasio reached out and took Nancy's hand.

"I'm glad we are friends. Someday you must come back to Copper Canyon and learn more about my people."

"I'd love to, Tasio," Nancy said.

Detective Garcia cleared his throat to get everyone's attention. "The photographs Bingham Stone took came out perfectly," he said. "One shows Dick Weston firing the shot that killed Bernardo Lupe. He will stand trial for murder and will undoubtedly spend the rest of his life behind bars in a Mexican prison."

Joe looked at Frank and gave a low whistle. "Not exactly the kind of place I'd like to be."

"He deserves the punishment," Frank said.

An awkward silence fell over the gathering.

"And my dad," Cory said finally. "What about him? He says he never intended for anyone to get killed, and I believe him."

"I do, too," Rita added in a sad voice. "Dick was always the crazy one. Marcus Weston was corrupt—but I'm sure he would never commit murder. At least, not on his own."

"He will still spend many years in prison," Garcia said quietly. "We are keeping his bodyguards in jail, too, and they will be charged as accessories."

Garcia turned to George and flashed her a smile. "And thanks to the photograph you took of the man who was following you in Chihuahua, Ramirez's agent has also been arrested."

Cory sighed. "I can't say they don't deserve it."

Joe put his hand on Cory's shoulder. "I know it's rough on you, and I'm sorry all this happened. But I'm still your friend."

"Me, too," Frank added.

George knelt by the chair where Cory was sitting and clasped his hand tightly. "Me three," she said, smiling affectionately at him.

Father Sebastien cleared his throat and glanced at Garcia, who nodded slightly.

"I spoke with Marcus Weston in his jail cell, and he regrets his actions," the Jesuit said. "And he recognizes that he must pay the price that justice demands. He has asked me to tell you, Cory, that he is going to have his lawyers sign the Double W over to you."

"Really?" Cory exclaimed, clearly surprised. "He always said Dick would inherit the ranch."

"Your father told me that he is ashamed of what he has done to your family name," Father Sebastien said. "And that it will be up to you to restore honor to it."

"Cory already has," Nancy said. "By saving our lives."

"And by saving the Tarahumaras' forests from further destruction," Bingham Stone added.

"Yes," Tasio said, stepping forward. "This has created such a scandal that no one will try to take our forests from us again—at least not for a long time."

"I'm glad some good came out of all this," Cory said, looking around at the people gathered on the veranda.

"Not just good things," Joe said, glancing at Rita and beaming at Frank and Nancy. He gave Cory a brotherly hug. "But good friends, too."